The Bully in ME

The Bully in ME

MG VILLESCA

GRELI PUBLISHING COMPANY

Library of Congress Cataloging-in-Publication Date
Villesca, MG
    The Bully in ME/ MG Villesca —1st Ed.
    p.   cm.
 Summary: While on a camping trip, Daniel, a self-professed bully who sees
others as weak, loses his best friend causing his life to spiral out of control.
    ISBN-13: 978-0-9827098-0-1
    [1. Bullies—Fiction. 2. Mexican Americans—Fiction.
3. High Schools—Fiction. 4. Death—Fiction. 5. Suicide—Fiction.]
LCCN   2010925625
[Fic]—dc22   CIP

Book Design Copyright © 2010 Raul Villesca
Edited by Stacy Kinney, Anthony Ortega

To our children with love,

Reality Check

The funeral is hard. The black shiny hearse is just ahead.

I still can't believe he's gone. The news spread like wildfire. As soon as we made it back into town, all our parents were at the hospital. My mother hugged me and wouldn't let me go until the paramedics told her they would have to admit me for dehydration and to stitch up my feet.

The cops came in as I was getting stitches and asked too many stupid questions. I answered what I could but couldn't seem to think. Mike came in and helped with the answers after a while because I had stopped talking. His father hadn't been called yet, but I knew Mike was worried about it. He didn't want to face his father.

I stayed in the hospital overnight. Somehow I wished it was longer so I didn't have to face anyone.

The next two days were brutal. No one was gonna force me to go to the viewing. My mom went, I think. I can't remember much but I didn't want to see his bloated face of death. I want to remember him just as he was two days before—kidding around with us and helping me bully those losers we seemed to have with us all the time.

By the time the third day came around, I could see a little of what was going on around me, but I wanted that desperate black cloak of darkness back. I didn't want to feel anything during the funeral or ever again. I desperately wanted to get away from coming but my dad was tagging along for once, so the alibi I was hoping for was not going to work.

The day is cold and rain pours like tears on everyone assembling at the cemetery. It's just like in the movies with all the black umbrellas and two black limos.

I have never been in a limo and wonder stupidly what it would be like. Maybe it has running lights, long leather seats, or maybe the bar is full and the glasses chime as the vehicle slowly makes its procession. Of course, Randy's parents won't be looking for any of that.

I know Randy's parents are in the first limo. I haven't had a chance to talk to them (nor am I looking forward to it) but I know it's inevitable. I grew up with them along with Randy. I will have to go and express my condolences. I just can't seem to do that yet.

My mother, father and brat brother, Luke, are with me in our car. I don't talk to them and I know they have their questions but they haven't approached me about anything since the hospital.

I don't want to have to explain over and over about what happened. I haven't gone anywhere in the last few days. I've stayed in my room, and I don't go out. My mom has come over and knocked on the door a few times but I didn't talk to her. Even Luke has left me alone and isn't bugging me.

Mike and Junior called a few times and so did Kenneth. Kenneth.

The thought of him calling is enough to make me start sweating with anger all over again. It's his fault Randy's dead. It's his fault things had gone so wrong. Randy would never have died if Kenneth had kept his mouth shut. Now he's calling me as if we're friends. I don't nor will I ever have anything in common with the pansy and I'm beginning to wonder just what happened after I left.

I know Randy lost a lot of blood but he was alive when I left. I took a while, sure, but I don't know what happened.

My dad parks the truck and we slowly crawl out of his beat up car. We have a long way to walk because there are so many people here. It looks like the entire city has come out for the funeral. People all around us are wearing black and white.

Why do people have to wear black? Black signifies death sure, but why wear it? I refuse. I have on brown. I'm not coming to the funeral to think of the Grim Reaper.

Most of our classmates are here and lots of teachers and coaches. Randy was popular and young. Too young.

I can't help but look around. Scanning my surroundings, I regret it instantly. Kenneth is here with his mom. It takes everything I have not to jump over the black covered chairs and knock him down. He should be where Randy is.

Some of the girls I've dated look like they want to come over and talk to me.

They better not.

I don't want to talk to anyone so I put my face down and don't look up until we get to the site where Randy will be buried.

It's hard to imagine that Randy won't be able to play football or go out on another date, graduate from high school and get crazy in college. He won't have kids or a wife and grandchildren. Randy and I talked many times about our kids and how they would beat each other up. I used to tell him that mine would always win at everything. Now we will never know.

Randy's mother is curled into her husband like a child. Grimacing in pain and holding her body, she seems to have severe stomach cramps. Her face is contorted with remorse and defeat. Randy's sister, Lizzie, steals a glance at me and throws me a small broken-hearted smile as she rubs her mother's back while squeezing the umbrella handle with her free hand and clutching it to her chest. Suddenly, she breaks down and howls with such ferocity that I have to turn away. The hurting I see is too much. I look down again and for the hundredth time relive his fall.

Part I
Before

1. Rules of the Bully

The street we're on is near the downtown area of Fort Stockton. It's a typical small Texas town deep in the heart of the "Wild West." The downtown area, as with many small towns, had hopelessly been rejuvenated but to no avail. The streets were deserted for the most part and this section of town always sits virtually empty.

The rain that had fallen earlier had been soaked up by the earth and pavement like a sponge, but that rock limestone smell lingered in the air. It's the one and only thing I've always liked about this place—that clean fresh smell.

We had come here to this strip of stores to see what kind of havoc we could wreak on the great people of this small pathetic town. We were leaning coolly against the wall watching what little traffic there was go by.

People always come back and talk about how great the town is, how they miss it so much and how they look forward to returning every year.

Yeah, they're full of it.

The town is about an hour and a half away from just

about anything, unless of course you count the great metro town of Imperial, which just sports one sad and lonely stoplight that is never working anyway. Odessa is the largest town closest to here and the steel mills and the trash littering that city don't exactly invite a flock of tourists. Fort Stockton isn't very nice and there aren't many things to do there except of course go to the movie theatre.

We have a movie theatre and at one time we had a skating rink (judging from the dilapidated building on the Comanche highway), but the attendance was low and crimes were high, so they decided to close it up. That's what the old farts that play chess down at the park say anyway.

Fort Stockton was an actual army fort a long time ago. It was also once the third largest spring water supplier in Texas. It has a little bit of interesting history but mostly, well, people come off the interstate to stop and eat, so I guess it's thriving. I think they stop due to lack of choice.

When you live in the middle of nowhere and are off of a big highway, there aren't many options. The only reason people stop here is to eat something, get gas, or, of course, take a dump.

Because of its desert location, it's hot during the day and nice and cool at night. We always try to stay indoors as much as possible, but sometimes, like this particular day, we had other responsibilities.

Who am I, you ask? I'll tell you that, but it's not as important as who I was.

I was 16 years old. My name is Daniel Vesta. Yes, I'm Hispanic and my mother is from Mexico. My father's family has been in Texas longer than Texas was Texas. My mother's family, on the other hand, moved over when my grandfather's business moved him here. Yes, they came over legally. I've even seen her green card. None of this, however, has anything to do with my wonderful personality.

I'm a big fat shaggy-haired boy who always took what he could by using brute strength alone. I seldom told the truth, was a compulsive liar, and said whatever needed to be said as long as it benefited me in some way. I had been this way for a long time.

Why am I admitting this you ask?

Because I know what people said about me when I turned the corner and they saw me coming.

On the contrary, I know what you're thinking.

You think I'm dumb, stupid perhaps, but I wasn't—I read. I've been reading since I was five and could easily complete complex math problems by that age. Ok, maybe seven or eight. I was technically the smartest kid in my school, even the state perhaps. I knew it, my teachers knew it, and I know my mother knew it. They're all very proud of me, but I tended to make that feeling last only a few minutes, if not seconds.

I read mostly about the terror of bullies and how it's wrong to do what I was doing—you know, things that interested me.

I also liked to read about psycho murderers. I know that's where I was headed. I kept up with the news. I knew what kind of background Jeffrey Dahmer and the like had. Unfortunately, my parents were and remain happily together. I had suffered no sexual molestation nor had I been mentally abused.

I hadn't killed any animals . . . yet. But then again, I'd never really had the chance.

I did have a tendency to lie, cheat and steal. I also had the noble honor of being a bully. I guess those things were in my favor.

What do I look like you ask?

Well, I did describe myself as fat and shabby (and a compulsive liar) . . . but, really, I thought I was pretty good-looking. I have blue piercing eyes, a roguish looking chin, and an overall debonair appearance.

Did I tell you who I was with that day?

No, I didn't. I guess I can share them with you. They were definitely and in no way more interesting than I was. They were what I affectionately called my "lackeys." Junior was always a short snot-nosed kid that looked like he got beat up when he was a child. Crooked nose, oily black hair, probably the scrawniest kid in school—which, in my opinion, explains a lot about his association with me.

We called him Junior because it is what I made up for him the first time I met him (original, huh?).

I don't know his real name, nor has he ever corrected me when I call him Junior. I suspect he knows better.

Junior always lived with his mom and step-dad. He is an only child, and often ignored. He never met his real father. There are rumors that he's in a prison somewhere in East Texas, but, who really knows? He could be a mass murderer or the richest man alive. My guess is that he's just a nobody. Like they say, the apple doesn't fall far from the tree.

Randy was another story. I actually liked Randy. Couldn't tell you why. He could be a jerk, about as mean as I was, tall with straight teeth, dark hair, dark skin, and, most importantly, a ladies man. Yes, there was something about him that made girls crazy for him; it was probably the jock in him. We played on the football team together, had both lettered our freshman year, and worked well together on and off the field. He was the star quarterback and I was the star linebacker. Girls loved him. Can't guess why; he was always pretty mean to them—even his so-called girlfriends. I have heard that girls like men to treat them like dirt. I guess that turns them on. Who knew?

Randy was tall and very muscular and way into football and basketball, or any other sport that happened to be in season. It didn't hurt that he was exceptionally good at everything he did and that we were stars on the football team. The best thing about Randy was his super hot sister, Lizzie.

Then there was Mike.

I'm not sure how to explain Mike, but I will do my best. He never says more than one or two syllable words at a time.

He just wasn't made that way.

He grunts more than anything else. Brown cropped hair,

built like he works all day (which he does, more on that later) and always wearing the same thing—jeans torn at the knees and a white wife-beater shirt. Well, to be fair, when we are at school, he usually wears a white t-shirt that says "So what" in red on the front.

How we became friends is a mystery even to me. One day, I just turned around and there he was. Didn't bother me much because he just watched when things happened or when we were otherwise involved in superfluous (learned that word in class) activities. He never actually participates but watches quietly in the corner. He is, on the whole, very quiet and doesn't talk to anyone, especially girls. I think he likes them, but I know they make him nervous.

That day we were near a new diner that had been refurbished in an attempt to revive the small downtown area. The diner sports a 1950's look with its black, red, and white checkered decorations. There are other small stores on this strip: a woman's clothing store that never sells anything, a furniture store that I'd seen one person go into in the last hour, and a bar down the street. The street parallel to this one has the police station, newspaper mill, and dry cleaners. These wonderful establishments have been here for as long as I've been alive, and, judging from my mother's old pictures, much longer.

This diner is owned by a fat fellow, ironically called Shorty, who every now and then would tell us we needed to leave. I knew he was watching us then. His beady little eyes were just waiting for us to cross over closer to his side of the store.

But we didn't.

We had much more pressing business to attend to this afternoon. We knew of a short puny guy coming in to help out at the diner with his mother.

He was just one of those unfortunate fools that owed me some money because he didn't have any when I beat him up last week.

As fortune had it, I had gone to the restroom after

convincing Mrs. Brasseuax (pronounced "brass – ho," you can imagine what we called her) that I absolutely had to go. She believes everything I tell her because I make really good grades. I don't understand it because of my behavior, but why ask questions?

As I turned to walk out of the restroom that day, I saw Mark walk in and stop short. I could tell by the look in his eyes that he knew he was in for it. He tried to walk out but I caught him by the collar. A perfect opportunity.

"Where you going, Mark?" I asked, pulling him back against the wall where I had a great view of the entrance—just in case someone happened in.

"I didn't really need to go. I don't have any money," he said, squeezing his eyes shut. Sometimes kids do that. I guess they think that if they can't see me, I'm less frightening or that somehow I magically disappear or melt into a puddle at their feet.

"You aren't going to make me wait, are you? You know how I get if I have to make you give it to me. I will not ask, just wait."

After years of abuse, Mark knew the routine. He would resist just a little—more because he wanted to be able to look at himself in the mirror than for my benefit. I knew what I was gonna get regardless, and if he wanted to resist just a little for himself, who was I to complain? I never cared as long as I got what I wanted.

Mark tried to pull away, grabbed my arm a little with no real effort, and looked at me with what I'm sure he considered his stink eye look.

With hope in his eyes and a little hint of desperation he stammered, "I . . . I don't have the money right now. I won't have any until next week. I can give it to you then."

We agreed on the place and I was gracious enough to let him out with just a few bruises. Hey, I had to do something to him. He couldn't just walk out of there scot-free. I just never worked that way. Most of the bruises I inflicted were always hidden in places people couldn't see. It saved both of us.

So there we were standing outside of this diner near a park (in case you missed that or are a little slow) waiting for this kid to show up when, lo and behold, Karla drove past us with her mother. She waved at us, smiled, and of course we all just nodded our heads at her (and the others tried to look cool). I, on the other hand, knew that I looked cool. It was too hard for me not to.

Karla is one of the most popular girls in school. She has the typical pretty body and pretty face. She's also definitely the "jock" kind of girl. She isn't stuck up though, and I think that's what makes her so cool. She has some killer blue eyes, deep as the deep blue sea. I didn't know where she got them because her sister, mother, and father all have brown eyes. Must be some sort of freak accident, but it suits her perfectly and she likes me. I think that was more important than her blue eyes.

"She wants me," Randy said as he reclined in a suave manner against the light pole.

"Nah, she only wants me. I saw her looking at me the other day at the Circle K. She's an intelligent woman. She knows what she wants," I said as I looked around the corner for that pip squeak kid.

"Humph." Mike grunted as he sat quietly on the curb.

"What? You don't believe me? I bet she comes back around. Better yet, I'll bet you five bucks she comes back around just to get a look at me one more time," I said as I walked a little closer to the entrance of the diner. (By the way, I knew she had to come back because they had just dropped something off at the one-hour photo shop down the street.)

No one took my bet. They just started kicking some imaginary rock around with their feet when the little pip squeak finally made his appearance.

Mark came dressed like a total geek with tan high water pants and a yellow button down shirt. He was the epitome of a momma's boy. You could see it in his eyes. He noticed us as soon as he got out of the car, said something to his mother, shut the door, and wandered over to us while his mother entered the diner for her shift.

"Hey Mark. You know why we're here," I said as I walked over to him with a deep scowl on my face.

You see, you can't greet them with a smile or a handshake 'cause then they'd get too comfortable. I had to keep them on their toes.

"I remember. I said I would have something for you and I do," he muttered, quickly glancing over to the diner. I guess he didn't want his mother seeing him give me money. I don't blame the kid—moms always give you grief if you're caught buying yourself out of a situation.

"Well then, how much you got?" I asked roughly.

"I've got thirty dollars. I had to take some out of my piggy bank," he said, taking out the money and handing it to me.

Now at this point, you have to admit he was pretty pathetic. Who has a piggy bank anyway? Do they even make those anymore?

Well, obviously, he did break into something because the money was all in pennies and nickels. Of course, money is money, but I do have my standards.

"I want it in dollars, go to the diner, and get it!" Like I said—I do have my standards.

He glanced nervously towards the diner, and I could tell that he wasn't thrilled with the idea.

"How about I get you some dollars tomorrow and I meet you here then? Same time?" he asked hopefully.

Of course, I had to say no.

"Nope, you walk in there and get the dollars. We don't have all day." With that I took a step closer to him. By the way, I am pretty tall for my age. Did I mention that?

He looked up at me and Mike grunted in his own special way.

"Yeah, you do what he says or I'm gonna show your momma what kind of gutless kid she has," Junior said from behind me—a safe distance I might add.

Walking toward the door to the diner Mark turned, "Well, OK, but you have to leave me alone after this. I don't have any more money."

"I say when you stop giving me money." I threatened him for good measure. I probably wouldn't bother him for another couple of months anyway. I gotta give him time to collect more money.

He walked into the diner while we watched from outside. He went to his momma and said a few things, which I'm sure, were a pack of lies. His mother smiled at him and gave him some cash. Whatever he told her must have worked and worked well because she was now looking at us with an adoring smile on her face.

Mark came out of the diner and handed me two tens and two five dollar bills. I snatched the money from his hand and turned to saunter away.

Over my shoulder as an afterthought I called, "Remember, I can be back anytime I want."

Already my mind was going over all the things we had and all the things we had yet to buy. Thirty dollars ain't much, but if used wisely, it could buy the right things.

My lackeys all got up and started to follow me across the street toward the park where my car was parked when suddenly I turned and called to Mark, "By the way, what did you tell your momma about the money?"

Mark turned to me smiling (probably from sheer relief that I didn't pound him in front of his momma) and said, "I told her that you needed the money to buy your little sister a birthday present."

"I don't have a little sister."

"Yeah, but she don't know that." Gotta give him a little credit, he's a quick thinker.

We crossed the street and headed toward the park and our cars. It was easier to walk across the street than to drive. I'd have to go all the way around the one-way path to get to the diner otherwise. Not gonna happen.

The park can only be entered from two directions. Portions of the park are one-way streets and there are nice newly developed paths for walkers. It is a nice park and one of the only reasons I think the town is not so bad sometimes.

It's a rather large park that used to, at some point, have a river running through it until the farmers to the north got greedy and wanted the water for themselves. So now all that runs through the park is the drainage from town. It rarely has any water in it because it hardly ever rains here. It could be raining in the distance, but water, for some reason, usually chooses not to stay here and who can blame it? Thankfully, the rain that had fallen early had stayed just long enough to make things smell clean.

There's a section of the park we liked to call our own. It's near a small community hall. It's secluded more than any other place in the park because it sits near a narrow street that is deserted most of the time. This street allowed us to practice our boxing, and, of course, the privacy to drink at will. It has one entrance that allowed us to see who was coming with ample time to prepare ourselves. The area also let us beat up dummies without anyone saving them. It was what I considered my domain and my throne.

The small community hall has two levels. The first level is situated on the bottom part of the hill. From what I can tell, it has never been used and I can't even tell you how to get there. The top portion is, of course, on the top of the hill and faces away from the park. This is the place adults like to rent for their own pathetic get-togethers. I liked the back of the hall near the park and the low part of the hill. You can't see it from the street or from the front. It is pretty secluded, so it makes for a perfect place to hang out.

"You only got twenty out of that kid? Had I known that, I wouldn't have waited so long with you. What were you thinking? That kind of kid never has any money," Randy said while we sat on the park bench and leaned on the hall building.

"Well, first of all, I got thirty. What the hell did you get? I don't see you contributing." I kicked the dirt with my shoes. I knew he was right, but I was hoping that the pipsqueak had been able to pull more out of his mother. But thirty wasn't bad and it would buy the rest of our supplies, mainly the food.

"Don't worry. I have more money to tide us over for the three days. We really only need to buy some food and drinks. We have everything else," I said as I looked around at the other guys. Mike and Junior were arm wrestling on the floor and cussing each other out in the process.

You see, every year around October we would take a camping trip. This was our fourth year going. We generally went to the outskirts of town and pretended we were in Colorado. We would build a fire, hunt rabbit and stay for three days. We never cheated nature one bit. I had to fight Junior about this particular topic many times. He wanted to bring his Playstation games, cell phone, and the small battery-operated television his crazy mom had won in bingo at the church bazaar a few years ago. I wanted to rough it, plain and simple. I didn't budge on that at all. We were one with nature when we got out there; hell, if I let Randy bring his cell phone, it would never stop ringing. His girlfriends called him at all hours of the day and night.

That was our time.

We were supposed to leave on Friday. We usually packed our things weeks in advance and I traditionally supplied the money, or better yet, the bronze to get the others to supply the money. Make sense?

"I found the propane tank you asked me about," Junior said as he got up from the ground. He dusted his pants off and added, "I think that it should be enough 'cause last year we only used half."

"Who's gonna carry that thing out there? I'm not. Last time I got stuck carrying that and all the sleeping bags." Junior whined.

"You can't complain. I got the grill and the lanterns last year," I finally added after some thought. I honestly couldn't remember what I had taken. I think I might've taken my backpack and nothing else. No one was gonna correct me anyway, so I didn't see how that mattered.

"Alright, who has the lanterns and the food this time?" I asked.

"I thought Mike was in charge of the grub this time. I did it last year." Junior was whining again.

He was truly a wimp. He hated carrying stuff and still hates to do manual labor. He wanted it all given to him which was why I always made him do most of the work. Sort of ironic, huh?

"Mike is in charge of the food." I took out the thirty dollars along with a little more from my back pocket and handed it to Mike.

"Ummhmmm." Mike said. Which, if you're paying attention, just means, "aye aye soldier: I understand the command and will carry it out."

"So, I take my backpack and the grill. Mike takes the grub, Junior takes the sleeping bags and Randy takes the tools we need," I ordered because I'm in charge.

"Randy always takes the tools and doesn't take nothing else, it's the easy thing to do . . . he already has the stuff."

Junior.

The whining was starting to grate on my nerves.

We just ignored him and continued to make plans. I let them know I was going home and would see them at five Friday morning.

"Can't I just take some tools? I think I deserve it after having to haul all that stuff last year."

I walked past Junior on my way out and gave him a good punch in the stomach that caused him to crumple to the ground. I heard not another word from him as I strolled to my car whistling a rock tune I heard on the radio.

Randy, as usual, followed me and got in the passenger seat.

I walked a few feet, then turned with a smile, maybe

more like a leer, "I'll see you Monday, and remember we're leaving at five in the morning bright and early on Friday. Be ready."

2. Another Day in Paradise

On Monday morning, I woke up ready for the week. I was so anticipating the great time we were going to have this weekend that I had a difficult time doing the boring everyday things. I was like a child with Christmas around the corner.

Thursday was early dismissal day, so I knew I only had to put up with this pathetic school and its overpaid teachers for three days. Yes, I said overpaid. What is teaching anyway? Babysitters who act like they know everything? I could never be a teacher; I'd come in with an AK-47 one day and I'd be talked about for years. I could see it already; the headlines would read, *Fed Up Stockton Teacher Goes Postal in School*.

Leaning against the hood of the car was what we did best, so naturally that's what we found ourselves doing that Monday morning in the school parking lot.

"Hey, I have a dentist appointment after school today, so don't wait up," Randy said, breaking me from the visions of me and a gun at school.

"You missing practice?"

"Yup, athletes like me don't need practice." Randy said.

I looked at him and smiled. "Athletes like you need the *most* practice. If you're like me, on the other hand, you don't even need to do nothing but show up to the games."

We were waiting for the bell to ring so we could be casually late, as usual. It was our daily ritual, I'd pick Randy up at home and we'd sit on the hood of the car while we watched other girls get out of theirs. A few times we pretended to have a smoke, just to see what the girls would say.

Randy and I tried smoking once, but we ended up throwing up instead, so as a result I decided my stance on smoking was that I didn't want to pollute my body. I love it too much.

Every now and then some idiot would park near us and we'd call him names if he was wimpy looking or a nerd, which in this small town was almost everyone.

"Hey, blubber butt. How ya doing this fine morning?" I asked Simon Blubermann. He, of course, put his head down and walked away. Hey, with that kind of name who could blame me? And things don't get better when you eat everything in sight. He had parked his hick truck a few cars down. That's what he gets when he parks near us, and he should know better if he doesn't want me calling him names. Typical wannabe redneck, but he falls short because he looks like a rat.

Seriously.

"I think the bell's gonna ring. We better get going." Randy was already getting phone calls and text messages on his phone. Girls called him all the time. I had eyes only for Karla and everyone knew it. "Yeah, baby I'll see you later tonight. Maybe we can go for a ride?" Randy sweet-talked into the phone.

"I thought you had a date with Yna tonight?" I asked him after we had entered the big double glass doors at school. That good old familiar school smell smacked me as soon as I entered the school. Our school is a 4A school, which means it's small but still a decent size.

The school is a one-story, broken-down structure that

should be replaced but it hasn't been. It has an atrium in the middle and is separated by hallways. Freshman, sophomores, juniors, and seniors each have their own sides of the building. It's not like we keep to our side and the teachers who are supposed to enforce the rule don't care. They usually stand at their end of the hallway and talk about their weekends and the partying they did.

"I do," he said, finally answering my questions about Yna. Smirking he added, "But I have to tell them something or they'll keep calling. Funny, they know exactly when Yna and I are together. They don't call."

"Maybe 'cause Yna's such a freakin' hottie." I smiled at him, and then noticed a puny kid walking toward me with a deep blue hat on that I thought was kinda cool.

"You know she's the only one who'd put up with your ass." I said as I approached the unfortunate kid.

I took the hat from him and put it in my backpack. I liked it and besides it might come in useful while out camping. The kid did nothing, of course.

"Where ya'll going tonight?" I asked, turning my attention back to Randy.

"Don't know yet. This is our one year anniversary. Nice hat," he said nodding to my recently acquired prize. I threw a wink at him and banged on my locker.

I remembered things now. Last year when we had gone out on our camping trip, all Randy could do was talk about Yna. It had become a little disgusting. "I'm gonna take out Karla this weekend."

"She know that yet?" Randy smiled.

"Nope."

Two scrawny girls dressed with matching mini-skirts and too much make-up approached Randy (already smiling and flirting). They had no life.

I rolled my eyes. "Shit Randy. I'll see you later; good luck."

The girls were giving him those looks they think are

sexy, but they just ended up looking stupid and sleepy. I'm not Randy, thank God.

I sauntered into Mr. Nelson's English class bonking some kids on the head as I passed them. I liked Mr. Nelson, he's muscular, very fit, and, most importantly, he doesn't talk down to us. Of course, this was something I'd never admit to anyone, but he is cool. He isn't married and he wasn't from around here, which is good but stupid. He doesn't have the small town mentality other teachers had. What the hell had possessed him and made him end up here was beyond me. Why?

He is built and he is a ladies' man. I could tell.

He doesn't give me any crap when I don't do my work in class. I always get it done, but sometimes I have other things on my mind.

Andy Wasterwill sits in the assigned seat in front of me. Another typical loser kid. You know the type: short brownish-red hair, freckles, jeans that never fit quite right, and shirts his mother picked out for him. I know he hates sitting in front of me. When they first assigned seats, he stood looking at the paper on the door for several minutes. Maybe he was waiting for it to change, but it didn't and I couldn't help but smile. The power to intimidate was like a drug. He sits in front of me and sighed audibly every time I called him a panty waste. I came up with other names for him like gaywad, turdburglar, proactive king, zit licker, crater face, pickle-weasel—well, you get the picture. But all he did was look at the clock every few seconds.

Time goes by pretty slow when you want it to hurry. After class that first day, he asked Mr. Nelson for a seat change. The teacher, of course, said no because Andy didn't have a good reason to move and "just because" hadn't seemed to satisfy Mr. Nelson as a good excuse. After that, the class for good ole Andy had become unbearable, I'm sure. He hated sitting in front of me. I'd put my feet on his chair when the teacher wasn't looking or I'd kick it, or call him names. It was great.

His monotonous behavior (learned that word in this class too) didn't fail; he'd put his head down in a book hoping, I guess, that I'd notice him less if his head were stuck in the book, but unfortunately for him, he was right in front of me. It was hard not to look at him.

I called Andy something and Kenneth, who was on my shit list most of the time, spoke up, "Leave him alone, Daniel."

"You gonna come make me, Wuss?" I smiled at him because that one usually made his face turn red, and then he would roll his eyes and turn around. Like clockwork, Kenneth did just that.

So predictable.

I laughed a little too loudly and Mr. Nelson threw us a scowl. I gave him a thumbs up and smiled. I knew the material as usual, so I didn't pay attention to the rest of the lesson.

I could pretty much do what I wanted. Sometimes a kid would open his big tattle-tale mouth to a parent or a teacher and I'd get in-school-suspension or ISS (which I really liked) for a day. But I would get out, and then retribution was mine. It would be justice time.

On this particular day, I was daydreaming about the camping trip and hoping it wouldn't rain.

"He wants the essay by next Monday. We gonna have time to finish this?" Kenneth asked leaning towards me.

I looked at him in shock. Had he really talked to me like I was some kind of friend to him? Amazing.

"You smoking crack or something?"

He laughed as if I had intentionally told him some kind of joke. "I think if we work on it tonight and tomorrow we'll be okay. Maybe it won't be so bad and it'll be worth it."

"You must've fell out your tree." I was still shocked. The guy had some *cajones* on him today.

He didn't answer me because the bell rang and we all got up to leave. The "Teacher Dismisses the Class" rule didn't exist in his class, so I easily pushed my way out. Other classes even asked the ladies to go first like I didn't have to use the restroom any more than them. Talk about gender bias.

I went straight to the restroom near the gym. It was

away from all the other teachers and the least supervised of all others. This was where we met everyday like clockwork before second period. We have health today. Our schedule was not the same every day. We had A days and B days with 55 minute classes. It allows us to take on more classes, finish early, or just take college credit courses. I would graduate from high school and enter college as a sophomore. It's a sweet deal and one I couldn't complain about, but I know what classes I can blow and which ones are important. Health was not one of those I cared about.

It was a joke and the teacher also teaches PE which is also a joke. The kids do absolutely nothing in either class. More kids are bullied in those two classes than even I could do in one day. Teachers have been told several times over many years about what goes on, but nothing is ever done. The principals were just waiting patiently for the teacher to retire and take their chances with the parents of the bullied kids, or the teen that gets pregnant at school, or the pot smoking…the list could go on and on. I've seen it all. See, overpaid teachers—case in point.

Mike and Junior were already in the restroom. Randy was always late, probably because of all the girls he had to fight off. "Hey, did you get the rest of the supplies I told you to get?"

I hadn't seen Junior since yesterday when I affectionately punched him in the gut. As usual he looked like something the cat brought in, his clothes were dingy and he smelled bad.

"Yeah, I got it last night. We're all set." He smiled and looked so proud of himself.

"Dude, take a shower, you stink and you better shower before we get out there. I don't want you smelling like a sack of butts and brush your teeth. You smell like you ate farts. Ain't no girl gonna want to kiss you. Ever." Shaking my head I stole a glance at Mike who was reclining on the trash can. Mike wore the same thing every day it seemed, but at least he took a bath.

Junior smelled himself a few times and I sighed as loud as I could.

"What?" Junior asked as if he didn't know but—well, maybe he didn't.

"I didn't know whether to give you a Tic-Tac or a whole roll of toilet paper," I complained, waving my hand in front of my face.

Randy walked in with a girl on his arm. "You forget something, Randy?" I said nodding at the girl. She laughed and patted his arm as if patting a dog.

"Beat it, tramp!" I ordered. I turned to use the restroom in the open urinal.

"Daniel, you're a jerk." She seemed to whimper.

"Yeah, and you're still a tramp." I started to use the restroom ignoring her. I heard her stomp her foot and walk out the door. Randy laughed pretty hard. I'm sure the dumb idiot tramp heard him as she left. She'd be back though. They always came back to him.

"I told one of 'the dummies' to meet me here today for a little amusement," Randy said. He hopped on top of a sink to sit.

By the way, we affectionately called them "the dummies" because we promised them things—strange things and they would show. For example, things like letting them sit with us in the morning (we didn't sit anywhere in the morning), walking with us to class, protection for a week, or a new music CD. Anything we told them, they believed. After a while you'd think they'd get the picture and realize we weren't ever going to give them anything we promised. The sad thing is that most of them are in my class and are pretty smart. There's such a thing as being book smart but not street smart. Those two things are totally different entities. One day they'd get it, though. I had made it my sole responsibility to teach them.

"Which one's coming?" I asked, not really caring. I was trying to figure out how to ask Karla on a date. I knew she'd say yes, but getting her alone was proving to be tricky.

"Steve," Randy said simply.

As if that explained anything. "Who's that?"

"You know, he's the one with the dirty blonde hair and enough zits on his face to work at McDonald's," Randy laughed poking his head out the door to look.

That didn't help me either.

Junior was getting that look on his face of anticipation (more on that later) and Mike couldn't care less as long as he could sleep for a little while. The blue doors and spacious interior of the restroom are ideal for pushing kids around and there is plenty of room in the stalls to throw some kid in and still have room to stand behind him. This restroom was larger than most in the school.

"Here he comes, Daniel. Do your magic," Randy said and rushed to hide in one of the stalls.

Steve walked in the room, stopped to look around, and turned around to escape. Since we've been doing this for a very long time, we knew the kid would do this. Generally, Junior would get by the door as soon as he came into the room because 99.9% of these dummies will put themselves into this situation before realizing too late what mistakes they just made and run to the nearest exit.

Junior easily got him by the collar and brought him (kicking and screaming) to me. I generally do the intimidating and Junior would flush them down the toilet or beat them up while we all watched. I didn't do anything but give mean stares; this allowed Junior to do what he liked most—the physical stuff.

"My, my, my, what do we have here? Scuba Steve, right?" I said. I grabbed him from Junior and pushed him against one of the sinks. With big watery eyes he stammered, "I don't have any money."

"What makes you think I want money, Steve-O?" I smiled at him.

He tried to get away. I effortlessly shoved him back to the sink. His oversized red sweatshirt was probably not the best thing to wear on a day you were gonna get beat up. It was too easy to grab that sweatshirt and move him back to where he was supposed to be.

"What then, I didn't do nothing, Daniel," he whimpered.

My smile only got larger. "Steve-O, you look like you don't wanna be here. Hurts my feelings Steve-O."

"I didn't do nothing, though," He repeated.

"I know, I know. But you came in here and we can't have that. You know this is our restroom and we don't like getting interrupted." I said this in the softest, most patient voice I could muster.

I nodded at him, "Steve-O, we have to do something."

He put his hands up, "No...No, Randy told me he needed me to be here. He said he would help me."

"I said nothing of the kind Steve-O," Randy said stepping out of the restroom stall.

"I guess you're calling my friend a liar. Do you have the brain of a flea Steve-O? This is how we work: no mercy, no mistakes, no second chances."

A look of terror and relief swept over poor Steve in a matter of seconds. I gave him a few minutes to let the info settle right into his little head. He should know by now the error of his ways, but I guess it's me who has to teach him a lesson. How else will he learn not to trust people?

"See, Steve-O. The problem with this is that you know you're not supposed to be here and we know you're not supposed to be here and when my best friend tells me he didn't ask you to come . . ." I sighed as loud as I could and shook my head, "I have absolutely no choice at all but to teach you a lesson. "

I shoved him back against the sink when he tried darting towards the door again. Sometimes they think if it doesn't work the first time, well, then maybe it will work the second or third time. "Steve-O, where do you think you're going, my friend?"

"He did tell me to come and he said he needed my help." Steve sniveled. He was really pathetic, but I didn't feel sorry for him, not in the least. Like I said, he should know better.

Pointing at Junior, I said, "Junior here is gonna show you a lesson."

He frowned at Junior for a few seconds and probably thought the same thing I always think when Junior's about to have some fun. He's flat out scary and crazy looking.

"Look, I have a little bit of money," Steve said.

I motioned to Junior to stop and wait, "How much we talkin' here Steve-O?" Money is money no matter what.

He searched his pockets frantically. "I have ten, twelve no—maybe twelve dollars."

I rolled my eyes. "Is that all you can get? Or are you gonna buy some more protection?" This was sometimes my bread and butter. The "dummies" didn't want to get beat up and money was a very important aspect, so many times I had a pretty steady income. Those dummies paid me weekly to leave them alone. Sometimes I did, but sometimes I didn't. I always told them that I had to make it fair. They got what they paid for. Yeah, I learned that one from my dad. If you're gonna go cheap and it's a piece of crap, well maybe it's because it really is.

"This is all I have… but I can get more." He sniveled.

"Well, this will buy you a little protection for the rest of the week, but you still gotta get some kinda lesson." I had my standards. Besides, Junior was set to go.

I looked over at Junior, who he seemed to be reaching for something in his book bag.

"Watcha looking for Junior?" I asked.

"Oh, I brought something from home that we can use on Steve-O here." Junior held out a disposable razor. We had talked a few weeks ago about some dude who had passed out drunk at a party. He owed people some money, so when he passed out on the sofa, they shaved half his eyebrows off. He looked ridiculous when we saw him afterwards. He had put two small Band-Aids on his eyebrows. We laughed so hard that I think we embarrassed him even more. He walked out of the store with his head down.

"You gonna shave them off?" I asked Junior.

"What? What ya'll gonna do to me?" Steve's wide eyes got even wider if that were at all possible.

"We're shaving your eyebrows, Steve-O," I said holding him down.

Up to this point, he had been watching us carefully but quietly; now, however, he was kicking and screaming with all his might. "Hold him down Randy," Junior said, panting from exhilaration.

Then ole' Steve found some new strength from real deep inside and really started kicking us. He yanked his arms away and it took two of us to keep him down. Junior turned him around and kicked him hard in the nuts. I hated to see that happen to any man, but if you're gonna fight, you gotta be prepared to get knocked in the *cajones*.

Little ole' Steve went down at this point and stopped putting up any kind of fight. Junior grabbed the razor and started to shave off half his eyebrow.

As soon as he started to shave, Steve yanked a little, hoping for one last ditch effort to get away. Unfortunately for him, this made Junior jerk his arm and all of Steve's eyebrow came off in one quick swoop of Junior's arm.

When Steve looked up at me, he looked like some kinda mutant. He looked like something out of a Mad Max movie my dad forced me to watch last year.

Randy and I looked at each other stunned, but then we burst out laughing. That was something that was too funny to mess up. We had to leave him like that.

"What?" Junior said, starting on the next eyebrow.

"Stop, that's enough." I said, taking the razor from him and throwing it in the trash.

Steve fought us again, but this time we let him go. As he was walking, no running, out of the restroom, he must've caught a glimpse of himself because it stopped him dead in his tracks. He looked hard at his image stunned. Randy and I broke into a laugh all over again. Steve looked back at us and then scampered out of the room, bumping into the trash can on his way out. I couldn't imagine he was leaving for class. He was probably making a mad dash home to Mommy.

3. The Real Man

My parents are great people. My dad works all day in the oil fields and comes home to work on the house. My mom is the nicest person in town and works hard at home. The only problem is that our house has had many different additions to it. I don't even remember what the original thing looked like but I can now say that the house is odd at best. I'm not sure it has "flow."

For example, the house has four bathrooms. Why a family of four needs four bathrooms in a four-and-half bedroom home is beyond me. I say half a bedroom because there is a bedroom in the back of the house that's one-half bedroom, one-half pantry.

And then there's the garage that has six doors and one very small window. I don't even think it's a garage.

My parents call it a garage because there's a small broken down red car in it that can't be used unless you completely tear down a wall and get it out. My dad uses it to store things.

There's also a carport that has no roof. Maybe it just isn't finished yet, but I've heard no plans to complete it.

Then of course there's my bedroom. My bedroom is large with three separate semi-rooms. I know—strange. Let me explain.

When you enter my room, you can see three walls. One area on the left, when you enter, and two more on the right—all visible from the door. Confusing, yes.

What it amounts to are three separate semi-rooms that are all open to each other. It's an interesting room and I really like it. My bed is to the left on the other side of the left wall. It's in a cubbyhole in the large room. I have a computer in my room, a large sofa with a TV, and a small refrigerator stocked with sodas and turkey slices. You know, the necessities. I never have to leave my room because there's also a small restroom in a little closet-like enclosure that has a toilet. Odd, I know, but convenient. I guess it's a room you'd never have to leave. It has everything. You can eat, watch TV, take a dump, sleep, and all without anyone jacking with you. I call it the "Lion's Den."

All in all, my house is great. My brother's room is much smaller than mine, but I don't see that lasting much longer. Already I've heard my father talking about plans for that room.

My mother, on the other hand, is known around town as the Taco Lady. She makes breakfast tacos every morning at five and sells them till around ten. This is her way of contributing. We aren't rich or well off. I think we just make it paycheck to paycheck. My mom, though, can make a dollar last a long time (so she says). But I really believe her because we always seem to have what we need and that makes my dad happy.

My parents don't really know me though. What parents really know their children? Most just think they know their children but, in reality, most parents don't really *want* to know them. They would be disappointed, disillusioned and most importantly probably crap their pants if they were to *really* find out what goes on in their kids' minds.

After school, on the Wednesday before the camping trip, I turned the corner to my house and saw that both my parents were home. I could picture them already. My mom would be in the kitchen making dinner and my dad would be working on some new project in the shed/garage type room in the back of the house. He had some really cool gadgets there. He even has a welding machine which I had just recently learned to use.

My brother was probably in his room writing something or drawing. He's such a dweeb. Short for his age, he can sit in his small miniature chair for hours drawing or writing. He has some crazy notion he's going to become the next Stephen King or create the next superhero. He has no friends that I know of and as far as I can tell, he doesn't have any other hobbies or interests. He is completely uninteresting, unlike myself. He has boring brown eyes, brown hair and a lanky body. No muscle.

I stepped into my house and put the groceries I bought using some kid's generous (if reluctant) contribution from last week on the table. I knew we would need some more sodas and snacks, but we'd get those tomorrow night. I was in a pretty good mood and, as predicted, my mom was cooking dinner in the kitchen while my dad slaved away in the shed. My brother, on the other hand, was watching television in the living room.

"Hey, looks like a bad storm this weekend," Luke said to me as I sat down on the sofa.

"What do you know?" I took his drink and chips from him. I firmly believe in being consistent. I was always fairly mean to him and I never said anything to him that could be even remotely considered kind.

"Just thought you'd like to know what you and the villains are in for this weekend."

After all the beatings he'd taken, he never learned to show respect or to keep his mouth shut.

He got up, walked over to the TV, and turned up the volume. I picked up a pillow and threw it at him as the meteorologist explained the highs and the lows of the weekend weather. I tuned the TV out completely and looked around the living room. My mom wanted the inside of the house to remind her of a cabin we had stayed in during one of our vacations. It has a "rustic" Texas look to it. She has Texas themed artwork throughout the living room, dining room, and the hallway. The hardwood floors are my favorite. I could really get a pounding in on my brother with their help.

"I bet you'll get rained on this weekend," He said again. He knew just what to do to ensure a beating. I walked over to him and wrestled him down to the floor.

"Mooom!" he yelled when he knew the beating was only going to get worse.

I casually let him go. I respected my mom above all others. Besides, if I didn't listen, she'd tell dad. But it was her mean pinch and stare that could frighten anyone. She could be ruthless with her punishments. Besides, I was leaving tomorrow for the trip and didn't want anything messing that up. As for the weather, I once saw the entire state of Texas covered by clouds on TV and there was a small dot that had no clouds whatsoever. I walked outside to find not a cloud in sight. That's Fort Stockton; it never rains here. Well, to be fair we do occasionally get a storm, but they never last very long.

"Don't you wanna go wash your face, buttface? Just remember which one it is."

"Funny, can't you think of something else to say? You always come up with the same thing," he said, growing stronger by the moment as he made his way to the kitchen. In the back of his mind, I think he knew I was leaving for my trip and I didn't want to do anything that would make Mom and Dad not let me go. He had gotten so brave today. That had to be the explanation for it.

"You can't stand behind her skirts all night, Buttface." There was no way I was letting him go with this one. He obviously needed to be taught a lesson, one he wouldn't soon forget. I guess he hadn't had a good butt-whipping in a few weeks. I'd been so busy preparing for the camping trip and getting funding, that I guess I'd been neglecting responsibilities at home.

The smell of fresh tortillas filled the house and got

stronger as I approached the kitchen. My mother was a sweet woman. So unlike myself and my dad. She was wearing her apron over her cotton red dress. It was her favorite. She's tall and thin and looks much younger than my father, which is ironic because she has five years on him. She has wavy black hair and always smells like vanilla lotion.

I took a glance at the food and realized she'd made my favorit—tacos and chalupas.

She was dressed in her favorite dress and she'd made my favorite food…

Something was up.

"Hi Mom!" I said, getting my hands on a fresh tortilla. I reached over to the refrigerator and grabbed some butter. Sitting down on the stool on the other side of her, I asked the question, "So what's the special occasion?"

"Aye, Mijo. I know you're leaving in the morning and I just wanted to make sure you leave on a full stomach." *Mijo*, or my son, is what she calles me all the time. She handed me a butter knife from the drawer.

Our kitchen is large.

I don't think it used to be, but as I said before, my dad likes to add on to the house. So we have a desk area for my mom, an island, and a bar all in the kitchen. My mother looked at several magazines before settling on this one. I think she really likes it because she's always in there.

I think it's her favorite room to be in. I hardly ever see her watching television.

As I buttered my tortilla and stole a glance at my brother who was also doing the same, I asked, "Is everything ready? I want to leave first thing Friday morning and I want to make sure everything is ready. Hey Buttface! Don't eat more than one! Those are for our trip." I started to yell as soon as I noticed him making a grab for his second tortilla.

He must've inhaled the first one. I hadn't even taken a bite out of mine yet.

I personally thought he was trying to do that on purpose.

If he only knew what was in store for him tonight, he would be apologizing on his hands and knees. He'd be serving me my tortillas *and* a plate of tacos in hopes that I would be easy on him. Instead, he was just making things worse. I'm not sure if all brothers are as dense as mine is, but he really was asking for it.

"You know your brother is old enough to go with you," my mom said as she stirred the beans and rice.

"Mom! I already told you. I'm not taking *her*."

"Him!" my brother yelled, taking yet another tortilla.

"I will not take *her*, mom. You know how *she* gets at night and I'm not playing babysitter to *her*." I pointed at Luke for emphasis.

As soon as Mom turned her back to me to stir the beans again, I made a movement with my hand across my neck to tell him he was a dead man and I was going to cut his throat. He knew what that meant. He just rolled his eyes, but I knew that had scared him. He didn't get anymore tortillas, nor did he yell at me again when Mom brought up taking him on my trip.

I know they wanted me to take him, but I wasn't about to. The camping trip was our time together and I wasn't messing it up by taking a kid brother with me. Besides, he would whine about everything. I don't think he really wanted to go with me anyway. He's not the outdoor type. He's scared of anything that crawls and doesn't like to sleep outside.

My mother always packs food for breakfast and enough tortillas to last a few days. Our camping trip was usually three days long. We don't have bears, lions, or the forest to worry about here in Fort Stockton. Well, we do have the occasional coyotes, bats, scorpions, and rattlesnakes, but they hardly ever come near anyone. We never traveled far and we could always see the lights of the town when we were camping. We generally hiked to the same place every year. We liked to take it easy, but this time I had a special idea in mind.

Fort Stockton is pretty remote. There aren't many towns near here nor are there many ranches. Once you're five miles out of the city limits, there's nothing but nature and you. That, I think, was the reason why we liked to camp. The nighttime is beautiful and every star can be seen on a clear night. It feels like you can touch them. It was, and still is, my favorite time to be outside: when you can feel heaven that close and smell fresh clean air and hear only the insects and maybe an occasional deer walking by. Yeah, I know I'm getting sentimental on you. Not something I particularly like to do.

Filling my plate with tacos and chalupas, I asked, "Did you pack our burritos for breakfast yet?"

"No *Mijo*, I'll make the burritos *en la mañana*." she slapped my brother's hand as he was trying to eat out of the meat pan. "Get a plate."

He scowled but listened and went to get a plate. My mother walked to the sliding door and called out to Dad to come to supper.

Typically, we didn't sit together except on special occasions or when my dad and mom were feeling traditional. This, luckily, was not often.

Today though, we huddled around the bar area and ate quickly. I wanted to go to my room and make sure I had packed everything. Every year I forgot something. This year I was determined not to.

I wolfed down the tacos and sweet tea and then headed straight to my room. I had eaten dinner without even waiting for my dad. He would probably say something about that, but I'd deal with him later. For now, I was too excited to worry about little things.

In my room, I found my backpack and began taking everything out. I spread all its contents onto the bed and began making a checklist. I wanted to make sure everything I needed was in there, and, after several minutes, I realized that I had forgotten to pack extra batteries for the flashlight and my toothbrush.

I made sure those items were in the pack then took the clothes I was gonna wear the morning of the camping trip out of the closet. I had been saving these clothes for a week to make sure they were clean for the trip.

Yeah, I know: a clean bully—nothing worse than smelly pits, crotches, and butts.

As I was rolling up my sleeping bag for the fifth time, Luke made another appearance. He was getting brave.

"Did you pack an umbrella? I can't imagine any of you knuckleheads would remember something so simple."

"I don't recall asking for your advice, nor do I recall giving you permission to enter my den."

"What?"

As usual, it didn't take much to stump the guy. He's fairly smart—just not street smart—and he's not really a leader in school. He's a follower and he reminds me of Silly Putty . . . you know, wasted space and easily molded.

"Get out or you get it now and not later. Your choice. But remember you owe me," I said, walking over to him as I punched my fist into my open hand.

For obvious reasons, he left the room without another word. I walked over to the television and turned the channel to a rock video. I like to listen to rock music. I really like the new music people come out with, but rock will never change. That's why I like it. Rock was the only thing I knew of that was as dependable as me.

My backpack was now ready. The only thing I needed to worry about was the food Mom was going to make in the morning.

I got up from the bed and walked toward the window. The moon shined clearly, illuminating the bare horizon. I only wished we could be out there right now. I walked to my bed, took my shirt off, and threw myself on the bed. I knew there was something I was forgetting to do, but I couldn't think of it.

Oh, yeah.

I was supposed to beat up Luke. He usually stayed out of my way, but he knew I would be leaving soon so he figured he could say whatever he wanted and get away with it. He was right, though, and I sat and pondered my options for a good five minutes before making up my mind.

I wasn't going to do anything that could jeopardize my chances of leaving Friday morning. But when I got back, he was gonna have hell to pay for what he'd done today.

I laid down on my bed with its denim comforter and fantasized about what wonderful things I would do to him when I got back. Maybe I could lock him up in the closet and say "Bloody Mary" three times while turning the lights off and on. If you've never heard of that, let me explain.

Saying "Bloody Mary" three times and consecutively turning off the lights is supposed to bring about a ghostly woman dressed in white with blood all over her body. According to some *reliable* sources, she is supposed to reach out and grab you, or worse. Luckily for me, or unfortunately for Luke, the closet in my parent's room has the light switch on the outside. I could easily throw him in the closet and torture him for a while, maybe put some Ben-Gay in his underwear.

Yeah, he usually got real scared about that. I could also stick him in the chest in the outside shed. He hates being in the dark. I could keep him in that chest for hours. I once kept him in there for five hours. I told Mom that he was at his friend's house and that he would be back for dinner. Well, he was back for dinner, but I made him promise that he wouldn't tell on me or I would put him right back in.

Of course, as soon as I let him go he ran like a bat out of hell to Mom's side to tell on me. I, of course, denied it all and admitted I put him in there, but said that I thought he got out and didn't realize he was still in there. Mom didn't believe me, so I was stuck at home and grounded for a week. Luckily, Mom didn't tell Dad what I did, or I wouldn't have been able to sit for weeks.

Dad's favorite saying is "you won't ever be too old to spank." Needless to say, his spankings make me feel like a kid, a nobody, a loser that couldn't stand up to his Old Man. It is the only time I really dislike my father.

Maybe I could sneak into Luke's room at night and pretend to suffocate him. He hates that as well. There were so many things that I could do to him. But tonight I was going to focus on the interesting nights that lay ahead. I thought of the manly conversations we always got into while camping and the hunting we got to do.

I only had to put up with the dumb teachers one more day and that was only half a day. Tomorrow we got out early, then we'd go out for the night, and then we'd be up bright and early for our trip. With these wonderful thoughts in my head, I finally fell into a fitful sleep.

4. A Night Out With the Guys

Early dismissal from school is like half a day of vacation. Parents are still at work and we have about four hours to do whatever we want. When the cats are out, the mice will play.

Teachers are in a good mood too, there's less work in class, and we get the rest of the day to really enjoy going out to eat and getting a little crazy.

After school, we decided to meet up at Randy's house. We had football practice together for a few hours and Mike had to help his dad fix a truck. I don't know where Junior had to go, but I didn't really care.

Even practice was a cinch because the coaches were eager to start their holiday. I left early because star middle linebackers only had to practice for a limited amount of time. Randy, on the other hand, had to practice with his receivers for an hour.

I love football; it gives me a chance to really pound some guys down. Being a linebacker really helps too because the harder I hit them, the louder the crowd is. It was great.

I went home to shower and change then headed over to Randy's house.

Randy's house is huge. His bedroom is like an upstairs loft. It overlooks the living room and has this wide staircase that zigzags up the brick wall. His sister Lizzie, as I said before, is totally hot.

I walked in on her once when I was a little kid while she was changing. It was the first time I'd ever seen a girl's boobs. She hadn't realized I was there staring with my mouth open. I was so awed by the sight that I didn't move. I don't know how long I stood there, but when she threw a pillow at me I realized I had gotten a full headlight view of them. She threw me out of her room, made a big deal by screaming at me, but couldn't keep the smile off her face. After that, I often took liberties passing her room hoping for another glance. I'd get one eventually. I am pretty persistent.

Her bedroom door was shut when I walked in. I couldn't remember the last time I'd rung the doorbell. I always walked right through the front door and straight to the refrigerator. After taking a drink and some chips, I went to Randy's room. It was empty, so I turned on the television while I waited for his return.

It didn't take long. He walked in with some chick on his arm. His mom and dad weren't around which gave him the green light to do whatever he wanted.

"Hey, Daniel. Whatcha doing?" Randy said smiling.

The chick didn't smile. Disappointment was written all over her face.

"We're going out remember? Just the guys?" I didn't want her even to try inviting herself.

"Yeah, I remember, but after practice Cherry here said she had something to show me." He leered at her and she innocently smiled.

Yeah, innocently. She knew what she was doing coming to his room. Too bad I was there.

I flipped the channels and made no move to get out of

the room. She sighed a few times and sat at the end of the bed tapping her foot.

Randy went to take a shower. He started singing at the top of his lungs, "You, you got what I neeeeeedddd!'

Cherry smiled. She should know better.

"He's not singing to you," I said.

She chose to ignore me.

"He sang that song yesterday to Yna." I figured that would get her going, but she didn't care. It was always like that with Randy.

She casually took off her shoes and curled her legs under her butt. I guess she thought Randy would come out and ask me to leave or something. She was in for a rude awakening.

After several more minutes of Randy's crooning, he emerged shit, showered, and shaved.

"You ready to go *Danielle*?" He hadn't even glanced in her direction.

I smiled at her. I knew Randy.

Maybe she thought he hadn't seen her, so she cleared her throat as loud as she could.

He didn't even glance in her direction. He got his jacket and walked down the stairs.

"Bros before Hoes," I said laughing and followed Randy out.

We went into the kitchen to make ourselves a snack. It seemed we spent lots of time in this kitchen. It was the first place I came—well next to Lizzie's room—when I was over.

"What time are the guys coming over?" Randy asked, grabbing a Coke from the fridge.

"Don't know." Nor did I really care, but it meant that we were gonna be there awhile.

Nora, their fat black and white cat came into the kitchen and jumped up onto the marble counter.

We hadn't messed with her in a long time. "Hey, how's Nora doing?"

"She's here," Randy said pigging out on some chips. We

had done so many things to that cat that I was surprised it was still alive, or even that it had enough *cajones* to come near us.

"She looks pretty healthy." I observed grinning.

Randy stopped eating and looked at me. He knew something was coming. He couldn't care less about the cat, but he was usually my mind of reason when it came to her.

"You have some scissors?" I asked him. I got up and rummaged through their junk drawer.

"You have something in mind?"

"She needs a trim, that's all," I said finding a pair of scissors.

I picked up Nora and chopped off her whiskers.

"Let's do an experiment," I said.

"Your experiments usually end in someone getting hurt. Well, in this case something getting hurt." Randy said glancing towards the door when he heard it slam.

Cherry must've finally given up.

I put Nora down and watched her walk around. "Whiskers are used by cats so they can judge where they'll fit."

My job in this place was to inform others of all the wonderful useless information floating in my head. "Let's see what she does."

Nora swayed a few times, disoriented, then tried to walk between the stool and the wall. She did not succeed. Her head bonked against the wall.

We both laughed. I wondered how long it would take Randy's mom to figure out what we'd done.

Junior and Mike came in shortly afterwards. We decided to go on the drag and ride around for a bit. We weren't sure what we were gonna do, but we knew something would come up. It always did.

The drag is a quarter-mile strip on the main road through Stockton. All the teenagers, and even some of the older idiots that refused to leave this place, hang out and spend hours going through it and around the Sonic. They'll park in places down Main Street in empty parking lots. The great metropolis of Odessa has a drag similar to this one, but, of course, it's patrolled by the cops because of all the drive-bys. We, on the other hand, don't have that problem so the cops pretty much let us park where ever we want as long as we don't have any booze visible.

The drag was already busy and people honked at us many times as we drove by them. Windshield wipers were no longer for the rain but used to wave at the girls.

Yna pulled us over in her Jetta. It was a smooth car and she looked pretty hot, but off limits. She was Randy's and had been for a long time.

Randy got out of the car to talk to her. Linda, her snotty friend, stayed in the car as well.

"Hey, you get all the stuff we need for tomorrow?" Junior asked.

I didn't bother to answer him. What for?

"Daniel, you get everything we need?"

I still didn't answer him. You'd think by now he'd get the picture, but, of course, he didn't.

"Daniel?" He tapped me on the shoulder. "Hey, Daniel? Did you get all the stuff?"

I belted him in the face, "Of course, stupid."

Mike didn't bother looking over at me. He continued to stare out the window.

After five minutes or so, I got tired of waiting. Some loser had stopped to talk to Linda so I figured I'd get out and face the drag. I probably would have tried talking to her or perhaps annoyed her enough so that she'd help hurry this encounter along.

I didn't have to though because Randy was already making his excuses. "Look, Yna. I promised the guys." He inched his way back to us.

By the look she was giving him, it didn't look like she was buying what he was selling.

She would though; she always did.

"Alright, let's go," Randy said climbing back into the

car. "She said Lizzie wants her car back. We gotta go give it to her."

"We'll take mine," I offered.

The ride back to Randy's house was pretty quiet. I don't know what Yna said to him, but it must've been heavy. I wasn't about to ask though; we never shared that stuff in front of Junior and the others.

"Let's go out to Suicide Run," I said. It was getting pretty boring so I had to save it.

The one thing I really like about Fort Stockton are the secret places hidden from "adults" and cops. We had wonderful places like Beer Can Hill (that overlooked the entire city), The Moon, (which hosted many fights), Knotts Landing (lovers lane), and Suicide Run.

This run is outside city limits behind the golf course and the coliseum. It's a steep drop that ends with a thick fence. That fence has a small gate that is just wide enough to accommodate a small car if driven just right through it. When you're speeding down the hill at 70 plus miles per hour—you better be a good driver to get through that one small gate at the bottom of it. This is why they called it Suicide Run. Hey, we live in Fort Stockton—we have to find ways to occupy our time.

"Yeah, but you better make it this time. You almost didn't last time," Randy said smiling.

"Yeah, I can drive if you want!" Junior said from the back seat.

"Yeah, like I'm gonna let that happen," I said glancing at him like he lost his mind.

Junior said nothing, but kept his smile. He liked this adrenaline rush more than any of us.

"Scoot back, Junior...damn, you stink," I said.

It took us a few minutes to drive out of town to Suicide Run. The mood had livened up a little and we were back to our old ways.

"Karla said she was gonna be out tonight." Randy smiled. "You finally gonna ask her out?"

"She might be that lucky tonight." This was an old joke between us. It wasn't that I was afraid of asking her out. It was just that I hadn't found the right time yet. I'd get there eventually, but she knew it just like I did that it was inevitable. No one messed with her or asked her out because everyone knew she was mine, so I could take my sweet time asking her.

"Last time I hit 67 before going through the gates," I said as soon as we turned into the coliseum parking lot.

"Nah, it was more like 62. I saw it. Try going 75. Maybe you can make that." I knew Randy was kidding me. He hated this run. He hated that second when his stomach dropped and mentioned it all the time, "I hate this fall."

"It can't be called suicide if it's not a hard fall. What's the fun in that?" I joked.

I stopped at the top of the hill. Randy held on to the bars on the roof we affectionately called the "*oh, shit*" handles. It was fitting.

Junior and Mike said nothing, but I could hear them shuffling to get a good hold on their feet. I looked at them all and we smiled at each other. I had to make it to 75 miles per hour. I turned and psyched myself out. I would make it.

I slammed on the gas and the car went over the hill. I felt the drop of my stomach and instead of tapping the brakes like I usually did, I slammed harder on the gas. The car careened out of control. The tail end of the car tried catching up with the front. I yanked the steering wheel hard to the left but the car did nothing. The gates and steel poles rushed towards my side of the car. I could vaguely see them getting closer through the corner of my eye. This was it; my mad 75 mile an hour dash had worked a little too well.

"Daniel!" Randy yelled. He suddenly seized the steering wheel and yanked it again and again trying to get the car straightened out and through the gates. He almost did it too, but my driver's side door smashed hard into the pole.

I slammed on the brakes. We sat there for awhile in stunned silence. Mike was the first to move. He got out of the car and ran around my side. I couldn't get the door opened. I looked over at Randy, who was still a little stunned, then he grinned at me. I smiled.

"Holy Cow! Did you see that?" Junior asked jumping up and down.

"See it? Stupid we were just in it." Randy said still smiling at me. We had that special connection. I shook my head, "If you hadn't grabbed that wheel…wow!"

It took us about ten minutes to get the door to open again. I couldn't close it unless I slammed it just right. Dad was gonna be pissed about that one. It was already a beat up car, so I was counting on the fact that it wouldn't be noticed. Well at least until I left in the morning. I'd deal with the consequences later.

"Yna said there was a party at the Rat Hole." Randy said once we were on our way back to the city.

"Let's hit it," I said still smiling.

The Rat Hole is this dilapidated building outside of town. No one knows who owns it, but it always seems to host parties. The great thing about the parties is that there's always sure to be a fight sometime during the night. It was great.

When we got to the house, the party was already raging. Lots of cars littered the street and the yard. Karla wasn't there and Yna had left with her friend Linda, so Randy and I stood around most the night talking to idiotic girls vying for our attention. It was pretty boring, so we called it quits before midnight because we had to get up early the next morning. The camping trip was sure to be much more entertaining.

I was right but in the wrong way.

5. Football Wuss

The persistent sound of the alarm clock woke me up at 4:00 a.m. I rubbed the sleep from my eyes and turned it off. I almost forgot why I had set the alarm.

Almost.

I jumped out of bed and quickly put on my jeans, red t-shirt, shoes, and yellow jacket. I firmly believe in wearing bright colors while roughing it. I read once that a kid had been lost in the forest for days.

The rescuers couldn't find him and the helicopter had passed over him many times. Because of the dark drab colors he was wearing, the helicopters overlooked him, so they didn't find him until it was too late. That was not going to happen to me. Not that we were going to be in the forest or anything remote like that, but it does pay to be careful.

I found my mother already up and almost finished with the breakfast burritos. She looked like she had been up for a while and her purple robe already had some eggs and beans smeared on her sleeve.

"Good morning, Mom," I said walking over to her and

giving her a hug. (Just a short one, didn't want her thinking I was getting soft)

"Aye, *Mijo*. When will you be back?" she asked again. She had been asking me that same question over and over again since the first of October. I don't think she likes the camping trip, probably because we were out on our own.

The first year I went out I was only twelve years old. We only went out about a mile, and it rained the second day, so we were forced to come home early. We were all disappointed. That first time, it was just Randy and Junior and me. Although we hadn't gone far, we'd felt at the time like it was the best thing in the world.

Like I said, we could've driven there, but we were trying to "tough" it out. Besides, I had just gotten my driver's license. A little late, but at least I got it.

Here in Stockton, seventeen-year-olds don't really get their license partly because of the lack of cars, but mostly because there isn't really a need. One friend with a car is all we need. Randy has a car (sort of), but he shares it with his older sister and until she leaves for college this year, he doesn't get to use it much. I liked going over to ask for it though because I got to see Lizzie, his sister. Like I said, she's a walking wet dream.

As I took a burrito and grabbed some orange juice from the fridge, I answered Mom, "We'll be back in four days. Tuesday probably."

Why could I stay until Tuesday, you ask? Well, at our school we get a week off in October. It's called our Fall Break. It gives us the opportunity to leave early Friday morning and get almost an entire week to relax when we returned.

The house was nicely quiet. Still sleeping, Luke and Dad weren't around. This made things much easier for me. I hated those long lectures about responsibility and honor. They got to where you started tuning them out. What do parents know about things anyway? Mine didn't understand anything about me.

What would my Dad say if I told him the truth? I knew

he wouldn't be happy to learn that his son is the bully of the school or that I stuffed kids in lockers, took their money, and terrorized them endlessly throughout the school year. It's not something I think he would enjoy hearing, although sometimes I think he hears things or knows more than he let on. He would ask questions now and then that would make me wonder. But I would never outright ask him and he never seems to want to know the whole truth, so I guess it works for both of us.

I certainly didn't want him waking up, hitting me in the head as he walked by, or staring at me with contempt in his eyes. Better to get out as soon as possible.

The dark lingered as I sat down on the bar stool and wondered if the guys were already awake and waiting for me. My foot shook like a dog after you give it a bath. I couldn't seem to sit still, so I got up and started to pace back and forth hoping my mother would get the picture and work faster. When she finally finished the last burrito, I grabbed them up and hurried out the door.

She took the pans and the dishes to the sink. "Wait *Mijo*, aren't you going to wait for your dad to wake up? You can wait a few minutes. I think you can wait. You're going to be gone for four days. What's your hurry?"

I didn't even miss a step. I took off out the door and pretended not to hear her. I could be delayed for at least an hour if I went back. I heard her sigh and that gave me a smile. I knew she had given up and wouldn't come after me. I was home free.

* * *

The morning was brisk and dry. The sun had not yet emerged which made the morning that much colder. There were no clouds in sight and I wondered for the hundredth time who gave out degrees to the weathermen.

They were never right and when they were, it really amounted to just a lucky guess. If you guess something everyday of the year, you have a fifty-fifty chance of getting it right.

Rain or no rain. 50/50/90 rule—a fifty percent chance they could be either right or wrong and ninety percent of the time they were wrong—this rule we quoted daily.

How hard can that be? But the weathermen seemed to guess wrong more times than not and, anyway, today I was glad. It was going to be a great day.

I rounded the corner at the park and a slow smile flitted across my face. They were all already there waiting for my arrival. They were arguing and fighting about who was taking what, but it looked like all our necessities were there and that was more important.

Randy, of course, wore his "roughing it" gear—a heavy brown jacket, jeans, work boots, and a yellow t-shirt. I guess Randy and I had read the same book, although I doubted it because I don't think Randy even knows how to read.

Seriously.

I'd never seen him pick up a book; I'd never even seen him with books for that matter. Randy was a great football, soccer, and basketball player, which, in my opinion, made him ineligible to be given schoolwork. I'd seen him hand things to other girls, usually cheerleaders. I always figured they did the work for him. I knew that if I were in his situation I would make all those girls do my homework and then do me. That's personally what I would do.

Junior walked over to me, so I took a good look at his clothes and noticed that he seemed to be wearing the same thing he had on yesterday and again I wondered if he even takes baths. It's not that he stunk today or anything; it just seemed to me that he never changed clothes. Which was gross. (I know: a clean bully.)

Mike was again wearing his usual wife-beater t-shirt with his jacket slung over his shoulders. He wore jeans, a cap, and steel-toe boots.

They all had the backpacks we bought together at the local sports store. We had to beat up a few kids to get the money for those. I think it took us over a month. But we were on a mission. We also bought some of the pots and pans that we were bringing along on this trip. I think I was more excited about using the new tools. (Yeah right, the camping trip was about the freedom to say anything and act like real men.)

"Hey, do you have the burritos?" Randy asked as soon as he spotted me.

"Is that all I am to you? A free meal?" I said in good spirits. I dug through the bag and tossed a burrito to each one of them. "So where are we heading this time?"

With his mouth full, Junior grunted, "I thought we'd go the same place we went last year. Why? You gonna change it?"

"I thought maybe we'd do something different this time. We could go towards that plateau we're always talking about."

Since we started going on these trips, we always talked about the different places we wanted to go the following year but so far that was all it was—talk.

Not this year—I wanted to go to the farthest plateau we could see. I estimated that it was probably around five to six miles away from our usual spot and would take us an entire day just to get there.

"This year we go to the plateau we always talk about," I said as I started walking toward the street. I didn't hear anyone coming after me, so I turned to see what the hold up was. They hadn't moved and they were staring at each other. I knew something was up.

"What?" I asked.

"We're waiting for someone," Randy said, adding quickly, " I just invited him and I didn't think you'd mind. I kinda felt sorry for the guy because his girl just dumped him. He won't bother you at all and he'll bring some food and supplies so we don't have to worry about him. It just came out and I asked him to come and then he said yes. I didn't think he would actually say yes."

Those were the most coherent sentences I think I ever heard him say. I knew he was rambling now and he kept going on and on and I just started to tune him out. I couldn't imagine him inviting someone to our special camping trip. We all looked forward to going every year.

My only question to him when I looked up was, "Who did you invite?"

Randy kicked a rock on the ground, looked around, and sighed. I knew at that moment that I wasn't going to like his answer. The expression he had on his face told it all.

Suddenly I became very angry, "Who the hell did you invite?"

"Kenneth," Randy said as he turned his head away and closed his eyes. Again, I guess they think I'll disappear or they'll open their eyes and it'll have all cleared itself up. Things just don't happen that way.

All I could think about was a stout pig-looking kid that thought he was a gift from the heavens. I once saw Kenneth with his head stuck in his locker staring at himself in a mirror for about twenty minutes.

I could see him from my desk near the door. I finally asked to go to the bathroom and went straight to him, shoved him out of the way, and punched the mirror. We didn't say anything to each other. He stared at the shattered mirror and I got this self-satisfied look that I kept throughout the day. I guess he knew better than to say anything.

I couldn't believe I was going to have to put up with this guy for three entire days. "Is he bringing his mirror?"

"Look Daniel, I know what you think. He won't bother you and he needs a friend," Randy said.

"I don't care what he needs. What I need is for this to be just us like it always is."

"I told you he wouldn't bother you. Maybe he won't come; he knows how you feel about him."

"Obviously he doesn't or he wouldn't have agreed to come," I said stepping a little closer to him.

"I told you he might not come. It'll be fine. You'll see," Randy said.

"Does anyone here want him to come?" I asked addressing the other two.

"Humph," Mike said as usual. Which translates to him not caring one way or the other.

"Can he carry all this stuff?" Junior asked with hope in his eyes.

"I didn't ask you all that. I don't want anyone else to go," I argued.

"He could carry all this stuff and maybe he knows how to cook or can shoot real good," Junior said.

"You're just thinking of the things he can do for you. You're not thinking about the whole concept," I yelled at him.

"I knew you were going to get like this. That's why I didn't tell you," Randy said.

"How long did you know about this? What were you thinking and if you *knew* I was gonna get pissed off then why'd you tell him about it?" I yelled into Randy's face as I approached him.

Randy was the only one that wouldn't back down or get scared of me. We had never actually fought. Sure we had our disagreements like every one else, but we had never gotten into anything serious—until now.

"I don't care what you told him. If he gets here, tell him to leave," I yelled at him pointing my finger toward his face.

Slapping it away, Randy said, "NO, I won't!"

"Yes, you will and if you don't, I will!"

"What the hell do you think you're doing?" Randy asked as I turned to walk away. "It's time to leave, and I'm going. With or without you." I couldn't believe that he had invited someone—and not just anyone, but Kenneth, the biggest wuss of all.

"Hey, Kenneth!" Junior said cheerily as if nothing had been going on.

I turned quickly to see the ignorant fool. I guess I'm not as scary a bully as I thought I was. I might have to get a little meaner when I go back to school on Monday. As I said, I have my standards and a reputation to uphold.

"Hey Daniel," Kenneth said a little nervously. I could tell he was worried about my reaction. He was right to be.

I gave him a slight manly nod like a fighter gives the man he'll soon be fighting. It wasn't a cordial look nor was it a "be my friend" look. I could see the nod had troubled him. I saw the nervous look he sent to Randy. Man, I hoped I'd never get that pathetic.

"We were just talking about where we are going. Daniel wants to go over to the second plateau we can see from our normal place," Randy said trying to make things a little lighter. But then he gave me this pleading look that told me he obviously wanted Kenneth to go. I shrugged my shoulders as if to say, "What the hell."

I turned to walk away. "We're going to be late. I wanna get there as soon as we can."

Giving Kenneth more than his share of supplies, Junior said, "Hey, Kenneth you can help carry some of this stuff." Junior didn't wait for a reply, he just started handing things, the heavy things, over to Kenneth. All Kenneth could do was grab them or they would have fallen to the ground.

I sighed real loud and gave Junior a knowing look. What could I do though? I didn't care what Junior did. More power to him if he can get some slacker to do what he wanted. I already had mine.

We walked out of Fort Stockton just as the sun started to go up, which was perfect timing because the wind had started to cut a little and there was nothing to protect us. We could have driven closer to where we were going, but we had had a long heated discussion about driving two years before. We had finally decided that walking was the best "manly" way to get there—so we walk.

The terrain out here is very cruel and there are no trees. The only things that can pass as trees are the mesquite trees/shrubs that grow a little bigger in some places. Shrubs, cactus and limestone rock are the only things you can see for miles except, of course, the plateaus and mesas that pop up every now and then.

There are enormous boulder-like rocks that jut out of the ground around the top of the plateaus that make them look bigger. The enormous limestone rocks, along with the mesquite, give off a wonderful aroma that can't be beat, especially when the rain comes. It's a smell that many visitors comment on when they come to the little shops in the downtown area.

I always wore boots on these trips because of the rattlesnakes and the scorpions that are frequently found here. I looked around to see if the others had followed my orders and everyone had on boots but that stupid Kenneth kid. We shouldn't have brought him. I realized that I would be telling myself the same thing for the next four days. I just hoped he didn't mess things up for us.

I was deep in thought wondering whether or not he had brought his mirror with him or if he was just going to use our steel coffee mug to see himself (I believe in acting like true men and I read that coffee is one of the manly things to do when camping) when Randy broke the silence.

"Where did you decide to go this time? We've been walking for about three hours. We're almost to where we usually go. Are we gonna keep going?" Randy asked.

"I think we'll go where I wanted to last time. It's gonna take at least another couple of hours to get there. Do you want to stop and take a break?" I replied as I kept up the pace I had picked up since leaving town.

"I do," Junior said and stopped. Excuses and whines are all Junior knows.

I looked to Mike and he shrugged his shoulders next to me.

"Nope, you're right, Mike, I think we should keep going until we get there. We're going up that last plateau on the right. It shouldn't take us too long." I said and purposefully picked up the pace.

"Hey, Kenneth?" Randy asked, stopping and waiting

for him, "You alright back there?" Kenneth had been slowly lagging behind which gave me more reason to keep up the pace.

Panting and wheezing, Kenneth murmured, "Yeah, I'm alright—just keep going. I can keep up. I play football remember? I can handle a little bit of sweat."

I looked over and picked up the pace. Randy knew exactly what I was doing, so he started lagging behind with Kenneth.

Kenneth was in football right? So my pace should be nothing to him. But I couldn't help but feel somewhat proud of the fact that he looked like a sweaty pig. He was sweating like a marathon runner after running a hundred miles. I'll admit that we had been going at a pretty hard and brisk pace, but—come on. Suck it up.

Did I forget to tell you that I was a pretty good football player? Maybe.

I started playing long ago in elementary school with Randy. There wasn't much I couldn't do when I was little. It wasn't too long after my humble beginnings that my dad knew I was pretty good at the sport. We continued to play and we made the varsity team and lettered our freshman year. This, if you know anything about high school, means that I got my letter jacket. It was a blue and white jacket with a big "P" on the left side. Our school's mascot is a panther which I think is pretty cool.

My mom sent my jacket to the cleaners and had our last name put on the back. Yeah, a little corny I admit, but I like the way it looks and it's intimidating when I have it on. And the most important part is that it's a big chick magnet. They like to wear it, don't ask me why. Must be a girl thing.

Needless to say, Randy and I are in pretty good shape, so when I looked over and Kenneth and Randy were lagging behind, I smiled to myself. The fat boy was probably wishing he had never come.

Good.

I didn't want him to get any ideas. He needed to learn

his lesson quick and maybe, just maybe, he'd go walking back by himself. One could only hope.

After a few more hours of walking, we finally reached the plateau I had been eyeing the last few times we had our trips. I could see the small Pecos River in the distance and knew this place was going to be great. We could take a bath in the river, get us some drinking water, and maybe we could find something to shoot at there. This was going to be a perfect spot.

We almost hit a snag when we got to the site because the plateau was much bigger and taller than it looked. It was going to be difficult to get up there, but Mike saved the day by finding a different, slightly easier, route up. We were finally situated on top of the plateau and could see all around us. There was no chance of a surprise visit from anyone.

Last year, we were making breakfast when suddenly some guy walked up to the camp and watched us for awhile. I didn't know he was there until he asked what we were doing there. We all just about shit in our pants. Randy and I had turned quickly, ready to strike. He was more concerned than anything else. He calmed us down, but told us to leave as soon as possible. He said this was a prime area for hunting. I could tell he was a hunter because he was wearing the typical camouflaged hat, shirt, and pants. Maybe that explains how he was able to sneak up on us. I need to invest in some attire like that. It could come in handy.

He had a rifle slung over his shoulder and it looked like he hadn't bathed in a few days. We told him we were leaving that day, which wasn't true, but our answer did make him leave us alone. Because of that experience, I made it a priority to ensure privacy. I was going to post guards and the spot I picked out was a great lookout point. I even brought my hunting rifle again, but this time it was loaded. Maybe I could make Kenneth cook a few meals. Yeah, I could do that.

When we reached the top, I ordered Junior to set up camp while I sat down on a boulder to enjoy every minute the football wuss struggled to climb the plateau.

6. Cooking Scorpions

Setting up camp was hard work. Well, it was for Junior, anyway.

Getting people to do exactly as you tell them isn't easy. Things are never done quite the way you want them to be.

I asked Junior to set up the tents on the north side of camp to block the wind so that when we sat to eat and cook we wouldn't have the wind hitting us. Of course, this wasn't done. I threw a rock at him and made him move the tents, something that took him almost another hour.

Randy and Kenneth were supposed to gather sticks for the fire, which took them forever because Kenneth hadn't quite gotten his breath back yet from the journey and Randy babied him for at least thirty minutes which infuriated me and made Mike sigh—which I interpreted as a positive sign that Mike was on my side. Actually though, there wasn't a lot of wood to be found up here, but I wasn't going to say that.

I was in charge of setting up the gas burners, the lanterns, and other necessities for the night ahead. The wind was blowing steadily and every now and then the wind would kick up just enough dirt to put in your eye. I could tell dirt was going to get into everything.

We had bought a small cooler that we used to store our lunch meat, sausage, cheese, and other necessities. Okay, not exactly necessities, but what we considered things we couldn't live without. Mike had carried this.

We even had a nifty little insulated shoulder cooler you could fit a six pack in. You could sling it on your back and it would keep things cool for hours.

We got it from some kid last year. He had it on at a parade. He was probably holding that thing for his dad, because the beer inside couldn't have been his, but, hey, it was a nice bonus.

At that moment, I was pondering the question of who was going to do the cooking tonight. I figured we would just get Junior to do it. It had taken him almost two hours to set up the tent, so if he started now he might have dinner ready when it was time.

Besides, I was sure I could make Kenneth prepare meals later, but I wanted to test the waters with him first.

I spread out the lunch meat, bread, and condiments on a canvas we used as our table and called everyone over for lunch.

They were all too eager to stop what they were doing for food. We always bring lots of food, but it never seems to be enough.

"I want mayo," Junior called out as he walked to the canvas.

"You make your own sandwich. We aren't your slaves. Hey, sensuous get me a coke on your way over," I said as I sat down on the canvas preparing my meal.

"Sensuous?" Junior asked.

"Yeah, *since you was up*, get me a Coke stupid," I laughed.

"Yeah bring me one too, sensuous!" Randy yelled.

"Mmm hmm," Mike grunted. Which again, if you're paying attention, means me too.

Junior made a face, shrugged his shoulders, and yelled,

"Alright, alright, damn. Give me a break here. I'll just bring the six-pack over."

Kenneth was coming over to sit when I muttered angrily, "What did you bring? Don't tell me you are mooching off us already!"

Kenneth refused to say anything. He just opened up his backpack and started to take out some crackers and cheese.

Yes, crackers. Like that was gonna fill his fat ass.

I couldn't imagine how that was going to fill him up. Those things are small and only make me hungrier, so I just laughed at him. Junior, without knowing what was so funny, laughed too.

I looked over at him. "What you laughing at?"

"I saw you laughing at Kenneth," he said as if this explained it all.

I looked at him for a few seconds and just slowly shook my head. Junior was sometimes too much, and he always took the bait.

Maybe Kenneth felt the same. I looked around to see what I could do to him when an idea came to me.

"Hey Kenneth, since this is your first time out here you have to pass a "man" test in order to become one of us. We did it when we first came out three years ago, and Mike did it last year," I said.

Kenneth, wary of me already, looked at me suspiciously and then stole a glance at Randy. Randy, I guess, decided to let me have my fun because he said nothing and didn't even look up at Kenneth or acknowledge that I had said anything.

"OK," Kenneth said very slowly. "What do I have to do?"

I pretended to look around and think about what test to ask him to do. "You see that over there? You have to cook it and eat it."

Curiously, yet cautiously, Kenneth slowly walked over to see what I had pointed at. I could tell by his expression that he hadn't seen it yet. When the realization of what it was struck him, his eyes grew to the size of basketballs and he started at once to shake his head.

This, I knew, he was going to do, so I already had my response ready. "I know you don't want to become one of us. I can't see you being brave enough to do that either. I guess you'll just have to live with being a wuss all your life."

I knew my comment had struck him in the right place, like being kicked in the *cajones*, because his face suddenly turned beet red and the veins in his neck looked like blue throbbing rivers. His brown shaggy hair fell over his eyes as he looked down at the ground, probably trying to figure out what to do.

"Well, I knew you wouldn't do it. I was just trying to help you become one of us."

Again Kenneth looked over at Randy, and again Randy did not acknowledge him.

Pity.

It's what I saw on Randy's face that made me pause— but just for a little bit. I detected what seemed like anger and resentment on his face when he looked at me but he kept his comments to himself.

Junior looked over to see what Kenneth looked at and started to laugh. I thought his laugh had a hint of nervousness, but with Junior, anything he did was a little strange and stupid.

"Ooh, I see what you gotta do. They would probably taste better if you cooked them,"Junior said, running to prepare a pan. I couldn't imagine there was a doubt in Junior's mind that Kenneth would eventually eat them.

"Scorpions?" Mike said after walking over to find out what the fuss was about.

About this time, Kenneth really started looking anxious. I knew he was fighting a losing battle with himself. What to do?

Do you eat them and get sick to your stomach? Or do you say no and risk being made fun of for the rest of the trip or the rest of your life? I believe I would eat anything if I were Kenneth because I know me.

Luckily, I wasn't Kenneth.

While Kenneth contemplated his ill plight, Junior casually started a fire and placed the pan on the flames. "You better hurry up cause they're gonna get away. Then you'll never become one of us."

I believe Junior really thought Kenneth would suddenly become one of the gang if he just ate some scorpions. Or maybe he was just excited because for once on these trips, he wasn't the one getting picked on.

Kenneth still seemed indecisive, so Junior drove the first nail in. "I dare you."

I got the idea of the scorpions from a book I read in the library a few years back. I read about worms and bullies or something like that and felt that particular book was right up my alley. Although with those kinds of books, in the end, the bully usually gets what he deserves, or you find out that his dad uses him as a punching bag or something stupid like that. But since there were no worms around here, scorpions would have to do.

"I dare you," I said. I knew exactly where this was headed.

He hesitated. I saw it, as did Junior. "I double dog dare you."

I know the line sounds outdated and corny but for some unknown reason, it worked on Kenneth. Junior had to smile when he said this. Somewhere in Junior's warped mind he thought there was no way Kenneth was gonna resist those last words.

With great reluctance and trepidation, Kenneth finally got up from where he sat. I noticed the deep indention he left on the ground. Kenneth was a thick guy. Eating scorpions would be a cinch.

He went around a big boulder, trying to find a good grip on the sides of the rock so he wouldn't slip. I peered through the rocks to see if he could reach in to grab it when, lo and behold there were two of them!

The situation suddenly got better with every second.

Kenneth hunched down on all fours and struggled to get a scorpion out without getting stuck with its pincers or the tail. Every time he tried to get a hold of one, it would rear up and stick out its tail.

By the tenth try, it was evident that not only were the scorpions getting agitated, but that Kenneth was beginning to work up a mighty big sweat. Kenneth seriously second guessed his decisions, both his agreement to eat the scorpion and to come on this trip. This reaction couldn't be more perfect. I didn't like him, so I was glad to see that scared look on his face.

But Randy had other thoughts.

Perhaps out of pity, he slowly walked over to Kenneth, gave him a pat on his over large rump and brought a large rock high above his head. He smashed the two scorpions several times with the rock and meticulously picked each one up and handed them to the now terrified Kenneth. I'm not sure if Kenneth was thankful or upset. Maybe he thought that if he couldn't capture the damn things, he wouldn't have to eat them. Randy solved that problem with a swift blow of a rock.

Kenneth glanced over at me with what looked like pleading eyes, and I guess, he hoped I would change my mind.

Of course I didn't.

How would that look?

With certainty, I knew if I changed my mind the guys would think I was nuts or, even worse, going soft.

"Well he did the hard part for you. Cook them and eat them," I said.

"Maybe with some salt and seasoning they won't be so bad," Junior suggested, trying to make Kenneth feel better. As he passed me carrying the slimy things, the oozing guts fell to the ground.

Junior unceremoniously threw them into the pan on the fire and graciously added salt and pepper. He flipped the things with his spatula a few times which grossed me out a little because that same spatula would be used for cooking our meals for the next three days. At least a good scrubbing and Junior's elbow grease would make it a little better.

Junior picked out the scorpions and placed them on a rock near Kenneth. Pitifully, Kenneth glanced in our direction.

As usual, pathetic.

I could tell he was waiting for one of us to say something. Maybe something like, we're *just joshin', you don't have to eat them* something corny like that but, well, I took in the demeanor of everyone else. Mike looked up at the sky, and Randy took a huge bite out of his sandwich and kicked something near his foot. Junior stared at Kenneth anxiously hoping he wouldn't eat them so I could beat someone else up.

Kenneth took one last glimpse at me and then slowly picked up one scorpion. He gazed at it while turning it over and over again. He tore off the tail and threw it off to the side. He dared me to say something with his eyes.

I didn't.

If he could eat the rest of it, then one tail was nothing to worry about in the grand scheme of things.

Kenneth held his nose and stuck his fat pink tongue out to lick the scorpion. I clenched my teeth to keep my gag reflex down because seeing his tongue on that nasty, gooey, crispy scorpion was enough to make anyone squeamish. I'm not usually wimpy about things, but who would eat a scorpion? Well, sure there are cultures out there that eat that crap, but come on, we aren't in that culture. I wouldn't eat bull balls, which I've seen my grandma eat, much less scorpions.

"You gonna eat it or lick it?" Junior retorted a little too excited.

Junior always gets excited when something like this is about to happen to someone other than him. For example, the first time I noticed Junior liked this was when we happened on a kid in the park bathroom once.

Our favorite pasttime during normal summer days is the old (never gets old) dunkin' heads in the toilet pasttime. We usually perform this task on average about five times a week during the summer at the park or gas stations, and I never once noticed the evil anticipation on Junior's face.

I had this skinny little kid's legs up in the air while Junior opened the stall door. This kid (I don't remember his name even though he was frequently on our victims) was delaying the inevitable by holding on to the sides of the toilet so his head wouldn't get wet when I looked over at Junior while he watched—a safe distance away of course.

The look on Junior's face was that of sheer lust mixed with excitement and anticipation—if, that is, you can imagine that. His expression was enough to make me lose my iron grip on the kid. He didn't have the upper body strength to keep himself from falling into the toilet, so he fell right into it. The splash he made when his head hit the toilet was enough to distract me away from Junior's expression. I never forgot the gleam in his eye. It will probably be stuck in my head for the rest of my life.

That same expression was what I saw on Junior's face as he watched Kenneth attempt to eat the scorpions.

"Just give me a moment. I need to see if these things are poisonous. I took the tails off which probably have all the poison in them, but you never know if the outer body has any left." Kenneth desperately tried to delay the inevitable. I just rolled my eyes and started to get up and walk away.

"I knew you wouldn't do it," I proclaimed as I turned away from him and munched on some chips. The sandwich tasted great. Of course, the convenience of being able to grab whatever I want out of the fridge isn't available when camping.

"Alright!" Kenneth yelled.

He took a deep breath, took one last hopeful look at Randy, opened his mouth, hung the scorpion high over his head, and stuck the whole thing in.

Grimacing, he chewed quickly. He gagged a few times as he swallowed the last of it, but he was able to hold his vomit down.

I didn't think he would eat the first one, much less the next one, but he surprised me by taking the next scorpion, tearing off the tail, and sticking it in his mouth. This one was a little bigger and he had a little more difficulty putting it down. He swallowed it then opened his mouth to show me that he had eaten it all before he walked away like he was something. Junior followed him and I don't know what he said, but the next moment Kenneth leaned over and threw up all over Junior's shoes.

I laughed at them both because, well, it was pretty damn funny.

I looked over at Randy and he just got up and walked away.

"What? I didn't do nothin' wrong," I told him as I shrugged my shoulders and laughed. I gave him my look of innocence. I could do that quite well by the way.

I yelled at Junior to wash dishes and clean up while I got Mike to help me set up camp because sometimes Junior is useless. It was still early, but I wanted to start on camp before it got dark or we got sidetracked doing something fun. Well, I was only really worried about my tent since I had asked Junior to set it up and you can only imagine what it looked like.

After getting my tent up and making sure it would hold up in a storm, I walked away towards Pecos River, which I guestimated was a good quarter of a mile away. Glancing at Mike, who had begun to set up his and Junior's tent, I let him know where I was headed. Again, I believe in safety.

I couldn't believe Randy was so worried and upset over Kenneth. We've done lots of things to other kids worse than making them eat scorpions. Why all of a sudden was he worried about this fat dumb kid? He was a pudgy brainless football player. He was in no way in our league. He was useless, and he wasn't cool in any way nor was he someone I would give a rat's ass about. I couldn't imagine why Randy had all of a sudden gotten a soft spot for him. Maybe it was a sister or a cousin of Kenneth's that Randy was really interested in.

I tried to remember whether or not Kenneth even had a sister. Nope, no sister, but I did vaguely remember a brother or something. Maybe it was a distant relative—some hot babe from Dallas or Houston. I believe he would have said something. So that couldn't be it. My thoughts floated towards friends, but could think of no one because I didn't think he had any. Maybe he wanted help with a class or something academic. But Kenneth was not the sharpest tool in the shed, so it couldn't be that either.

I had been walking, lost in thought, for a while before I realized that the river was farther away than I thought. It was still some distance away. I know the terrain. It isn't much different from what you'll find in town in empty lots. Mesquite trees are scattered about and bushes and rocks litter the ground.

You do have to worry about where you're stepping. Small and large rocks are everywhere and there is this awful plant that grows here with three inch thorns throughout its entire surface. The plant grows into big bushes but it starts small and you could easily step on one without noticing until it's too late. Those thick thorns could go through most shoes and puncture your feet. Sometimes they carry bacteria and you can get seriously hurt. I didn't want to step on one and cut this trip short, even if we did have Kenneth.

Then, of course, there are snakes. The snakes use those same bushes to ambush their prey, especially at night. Big or small, I didn't want to be some snake's meal tomorrow. By the time they found us, the buzzards would've already eaten my eyes out. DNA tests would have to be done to identify me. Plus, the last thing I wanted to do was try to suck poison out of Kenneth's butt, so I made a mental note of making sure to remind Randy to tell the idiot about the snakes.

I finally made it to the river and sat down on the bank. It wasn't much of a river, probably only about three to four feet at its deepest and a good thirty feet wide. Not much, like I said, but, hey, it was a place to wash the dishes and it won't taste too bad if we're in danger of dehydrating.

I can remember when we were just learning how to swim and our parents would bring us to this river a few miles down.

We'd wade for hours and regardless of how much sunscreen our parents would smother on us, we always came home looking like lobsters and smelling like aloe. The ride home always felt very short because I'd fall asleep as soon as the car took off. When I'd wake up, we'd be home.

Maybe that's what I needed now to clear my mind—a nice swim.

As I stripped down to my boxers, my heart began to race because I suddenly, surprisingly, was looking forward to this swim. I hung my clothes on some bushes to make sure no insects got in them and I took the plunge.

"Oh, my God! Does this water have ice cubes in it?" I yelled. My family jewels had shrunk to the size of raisins. I was definitely awake now.

I had forgotten that the hardest part of swimming here was getting in.

"Hey, why do you always have to do that?" a voice boomed behind me.

Randy surprised the hell out of me, but, of course, I had to be suave about it all (even if he did catch me off guard). So I didn't turn to acknowledge him, but plunged down deeper into the water.

I ignored him for a while as he stood there waiting for me to say something. Even though I was freezing my butt off, I refused to get out. I tried swimming a few yards in both directions, which helped immensely with the cold. But eventually I couldn't help it. "You just feel sorry for him. I don't know what sob story he told you to get you to invite him, but I know for a fact it worked."

Randy crouched down on the river bank and took his shoes off. "I just think that if you heard what he had to say, you might lighten up."

"Now, when have you known me to be like that? I can't stand stupidity and I have no patience for it."

"Is that why you keep Junior around?"

"I keep Junior around so he can work for me. Nothing

more, nothing less. I don't need another Junior. I already have one." I turned on my back to backstroke.

Randy sighed and pushed a large rock in the water with his toes. I could tell he was trying to find the right thing to say to me. Randy was like that, he took his time finding the right words. He had a speech problem when he was a kid so he always said that words were important—the way you say them and the words you use. "Just do me a small favor and leave him alone. At least do that."

"I can't promise you anything, but it just goes to show. You shouldn't have brought him."

"Alright, that's fair, but next time you want to be mean to the guy, remember that he just lost his brother a few days ago. And his mother's had a total meltdown."

He picked up his shoes and stomped away.

So that was it.

I remembered some classmates talking about it a few weeks ago, how Kenneth's brother was a Marine and had gone to Iraq. Some roadside bomb had shattered both of his legs. They thought for a while that he was going to make it, but his brother had developed an infection at the hospital and it had gotten into his bloodstream. You can't trust hospitals, they suck. Everyone knows you don't stand a chance once something like that enters your blood.

I realized that losing somebody can rock your world, but everybody comes and goes. Life goes on; you dust yourself off and keep marching like a good soldier. When my grandfather died, no one was there to show me any sympathy.

Kenneth's just a wuss. What makes him any different? He was just another punk I dealt with on a daily basis.

So his brother died, Randy felt sorry for him, and I was supposed to show mercy?

Perfect.

7. Just the Guys

We finally set up camp and finished arranging our lunch meats (for the next few days) in the cooler. Mike had forgotten to put them in. Sandwiches, chips, and sodas are easy fare and not hard to tote around; well, not for Junior anyway. Kenneth had brought peanut butter and jelly sandwiches and some grapes.

Don't ask. I certainly didn't. It was just like the Lunchables.

Mike and I had taken our time to gather some more wood because Randy and Kenneth had been absolutely useless earlier.

Because it hardly ever rains here in West Texas, there is plenty of mesquite kindling scattered along the bottom of the plateau. We did a heck of a job gathering plenty for dinner. We probably had enough wood to last a few days.

"I gathered the wood; Kenneth, you and Randy need to start the fire and create a fire pit," I ordered. I threw the last of the wood we carried onto the pile.

Randy was preoccupied again, but I couldn't see why. I left Kenneth alone throughout the entire evening. I didn't even say anything about the peanut butter and jelly sandwiches. I should, at the very least, get a medal for that.

Randy rose from his position next to me and started to help Kenneth create a clearing for the fire. Together they made a large circle of rocks with kindling in the middle. Kenneth took out a lighter from his jeans pocket and held it close to a piece of wood. It wouldn't light. I smiled, shook my head and walked away. Kenneth was such a loser and Randy should have known better than to bring this idiot.

"Here, try using dead leaves and small branches. Light those on fire underneath the wood." Randy was being extremely patient with him considering lighting a fire was supposed to be easy for any man, especially if you have a lighter.

"Oh, I've never been camping before, so I don't know what to do. My dad used to talk about going when I was young but when he died and it was just my mom and my brother, well she isn't much on the outdoors life," Kenneth explained trying to light the stack of leaves he had formed.

So, not only was his brother gone, but this guy had lost his father too? Way to go Kenneth, this would be great on my conscience (if I had one).

"It's okay. I didn't know much either the first time I came out here. Daniel taught us all here," Randy said throwing a smile at me for the first time in a few hours. It really was amazing, the relationship between Randy and me. We knew and understood each other more than anyone else I know. I could always count on Randy to be there when something new and exciting was happening.

It wasn't long before we gathered around the fire to do my favorite thing when we camped.

We talked man.

Junior had been sneaking some of his mom's beer out for weeks to make sure we had enough to enjoy for our trip. His mother was very particular and extremely selfish with her beer, so he could only take one or two at a time until we had enough.

Hey, it was free, so we didn't complain about how cheap

and watered down it was.

As he passed them out, we stretched out to enjoy the beautiful clear night.

"Hey, Mike, I didn't tell you what we did to old Mrs. Putris the other day." I looked over at Randy and as he smiled, Junior started to laugh out loud.

"Who is Mrs. Putris?" Kenneth asked me. He actually spoke to me, I didn't know whether I liked that or not. In my infinite wisdom, I chose to ignore him.

"Old Mrs. Putris, or Putrid as Daniel likes to call her, is a big fat old lady that lives over on Mesa Street. She's always yelling at us as when we drive by. She forever sits outside on her front porch." Randy liked to fill people in, especially Kenneth, I guess.

"Anyway, Mike, we were riding by and thinking we wanted to see what she would do if we actually stopped. She didn't even let us get close. As soon as Randy started to push the brakes and pull up to her curb, she took off running after us!"

"No way?" Mike grunted.

"Yeah, and to see that Jello wiggle like that has been making me sick for days," I said. I pretended to gag a few times. See, old Mrs. Putrid has been a great distraction in our sad two-bit town; we get a little bored and someone will eventually say, "Hey, let's get Mrs. Putrid" or "Mrs. Putrid is probably really bored without us about now."

As the story goes, the lady sits outside all day just watching cars go by. Every now and then she stomps after a car or two and screams at them, telling people to get out or beware "the curse." She says that one a lot. Of course, no one dared to stop and ask her.

What *exactly* does she mean by the curse? We have no way of knowing what she means. She spouts out loads of curses and superstitious nonsense.

We found out about her one day by accident. Randy and I were headed to the local movie theatre—if you can call the place that. It only has two very old movies playing at one time, and the seats are always empty except for a couple of teenagers looking for a place to make out. The place looks as bad as it smells.

Well, on this particular day, Randy dropped something under his feet while we were on our way to see a movie. He slowed down and reached under his feet to grab it when his right shoulder accidentally hit the horn on the steering wheel. The next thing we knew, this little old lady dressed in a mumu and a dingy white sweater jumped with surprising agility from her perch on the porch and started screaming at us to leave *us* alone. Randy was so startled that he swerved onto the sidewalk and hit a garbage can. Needless to say, we tried going by there again a few days later to see if she would go at us again—and she did. She always seemed to include the *we* or *us* part yet we have never seen another soul get near. And so our weekly stops at old Mrs. Putrid's street began.

Randy finally joined our conversation to laughingly tell us how he didn't even get to stop the car. "She was really mad, or she looked it. I don't think I've ever seen her face. She's like a crazy woman. I saw her get close to the car in seconds and I thought she was going to hit us with that stick she carries."

"Yeah, she is a crazy woman. Maybe next time we can t.p. her house or throw some eggs at it. I bet she'll get pissed off at that!" Junior said, putting his two cents in.

"I wonder if there's something wrong with the lady or if she's lonely or has mental problems," Kenneth murmured.

"Who cares?" I asked taking a nice long sip of my beer.

I never stopped to talk to the lady nor did she give anyone a chance to. I didn't see anything wrong with driving by the house. The old, narrow road we were on was a public one. It was not as if we intentionally drove into her driveway or trespassed into her old dilapidated house.

Kenneth shrugged his shoulders and Randy just looked away. I could tell Kenneth's comment bothered Randy. Randy wasn't much on emotional mumbo-jumbo, but he sure was acting strange with Kenneth around.

"Why don't we show Kenneth our yearly science experiment?" Junior suggested happily.

Junior loved this part of the trip. He liked watching helpless things get hurt as long as it wasn't him. It was that weird silly apprehensive look he gets that I told you about earlier.

"If you want to do that, then you have to go hunt them down," I said as I got up and looked for the lighter and gasoline. We always stored a little fuel in a silver flask we found a few years back. I believe that it was a whiskey flask once upon a time, but we used it only for gasoline.

"I did it last year, so I think its Kenneth's turn or Randy's. Even Mike has never done it." Junior was such a whiner.

"You brought it up, you do it. You're the one that gets a sick thrill out of it." Junior didn't bother to say anything about that, nor did he comment on his own actions or feelings. We had been down that road before. He knew that I was a little fascinated with the whole thing, but I never once took so much grotesque pleasure in the experiment like Junior did.

I decided that the hunt for them was going to take Junior a while. "Take the flashlight—it's easier to see them that way."

Scorpions glow in the dark. Well, the light yellow ones do and there's always an overabundance of them out here, especially at night. We had begun conducting this little experiment after hearing a rumor about it. Randy brought it up once while we sat around the campfire and the next thing you know, we were all scouring the campsite for scorpions to see if the rumor worked.

It did.

I became so fascinated with the little creatures. In my own twisted mind, I revered them and I set out to learn everything I could about them. The way they're faced with utter defeat and certain death, yet remain in charge of how they die, is something that intrigues the hell out of me. They remind me of Samurai warriors or the Spartans of long ago when they faced Persia.

Lethal and honorable to the end.

"How's Julian been nowadays?" I asked Randy.

Randy laughed, "He's better—whatever you texted that day must've had an impact."

"You never saw what I sent?" Randy shook his head, so I filled him in. "Julian made us stay late at football practice because he couldn't get his fat ass off the line fast enough. It really pissed me off because we were all so tired. After practice, I stuffed his pants with ice, yanked them off, and became the paparazzi."

"You took pictures of him—you know?" Randy asked.

"Sent the pics to everyone I know. They sent them on and on and on. He didn't know what hit him."

"That's just plain shitty," Kenneth said shaking his head.

"No one asked you, stupid." I had every intention of hitting him in the head but then decided not to. He'll get what's coming on this trip. I would make sure.

I lay down in my tent near the fire and closed my eyes to rest. It had been a long day and a long walk.

I once read a book about a kid who chooses to be in a race with other kids. If they win, they have the chance to get anything they want for the rest of their lives. The rules are simple: walk until they can't walk anymore. There was a catch however: the military will shoot and kill the kids until there is just one left standing. These boys have to shit, eat, and sleep standing up. I remember the leading character gets to know the lives of the other kids in the race. He actually helps some of them. It's a story written by my favorite writer, Stephen King. He really knows how to make twisted and scary characters.

That story stuck with me because I knew that I would be the last one standing if I had been able to be in that same race. I would get anything in the world and I would be revered and admired by all. I wouldn't, however, make friends with any of the others, nor would I try to help them. That wouldn't help out my cause now would it? You would have to be crazy to help those you are trying to beat, especially if it meant your life could be lost. I guess that's why the story intrigued me so much, it was like a race for life. The scorpions do it, the Samurai warriors, the Spartans, and the long walk kid did it. All of them have something in common. They all shared a special bond with me too.

I could feel that my feet were a little sore. The day's walk was nothing, but I did feel a little tired.

Just then, I heard a distant, faint, yet unmistakable roar. Thunder.

I groaned.

Junior's distinct whine was coming from a few feet away. "I told you I heard it was going to rain today and tomorrow. I'm not gonna sleep outside of my tent, Mike. You're gonna have to share the tent."

"Yeah," Mike said not getting up from his perch inside the tent.

"Don't start, Junior. Just keep looking for them," I said, turning over to lay on my back.

I love the outdoors. That night, the moon was in full appearance, so I could see the stars hovering above us creating a stark contrast to the approaching clouds. The air had gotten noticeably cooler within the last few minutes. I hated what that meant. I didn't want to have to pack everything up. I can stand a little rain, but I was hard pressed to admit that I hadn't given the forecast of rain much credence. I mean, come on. We only come out here one weekend a year. It's not like we do it all the time.

I think it's all because of Kenneth: after all, this had never happened before. He was our black cloud. I looked over to see Randy and Kenneth talking quietly in the tent they were sharing.

Again, I felt betrayed. Randy wouldn't be over there with that fat pig if Kenneth had the good sense to stay away. I guess I was right. Maybe I am going soft. People have to be reminded again and again of what I'm capable of. I would show him and Randy tomorrow. I would show them that I was to be feared and admired, revered.

It better not rain.

It wouldn't rain. It wouldn't dare.

"I found some!" Junior yelled across our campsite.

8. The Ring of Fire

Junior was so wound up. I knew he had found a few. It had only taken about an hour to collect five scorpions. I heard the roar of the thunder again, but it sounded far away so I knew we would have plenty of time to complete our little science experiment.

I haven't quite told you the particulars have I? Call it suspense, no maybe mystery.

Ever since Randy brought it up a few years ago, we have performed this little experiment.

That is (I believe) what labs are for: to prove that things aren't gonna come out the way you would normally expect.

Take Junior, for example. Say you've spent nine months hoping to have a healthy, smart, and highly intelligent baby. A baby who will one day grow up to become a scientist, a lawyer, a doctor, hell maybe even the next President of the United States. You would at the very least hope that the baby would be normal or a responsible adult.

Then you go and have something like Junior.

He's what experiments are designed for because once there's proof of how things can go so horribly wrong, there is no way that those poor pathetic parents are going to try again.

Thus.

Junior—an only child.

See? So we have been hoping to prove this theory about scorpions incorrect, but so far we haven't been successful.

I got the flask and a lighter, made a deep circle in the ground with my shoe, and waited for everyone to come and see.

"What are ya'll doing?" Kenneth said, walking suspiciously to where we were standing. He probably thought we were going to make him eat them again. I'm surprised Randy didn't tell him while they were over there hunched over talking privately.

I, of course, ignored him and so did everyone else. Once we got started, it would be pretty obvious what we were going to do.

As soon as I had the circle dug fairly deep, I looked over at Junior. He nodded in understanding that I was ready.

I poured the gasoline into the circle and lit it on fire just after Junior poured the scorpions into the circle.

The circle was blazing as the scorpions raced around frantically looking for an escape. It didn't take long. One scorpion moved around, stopped for a few seconds, and stabbed itself with its tail in the head.

"Holy crap!" Kenneth looked away as the other scorpions did the same. One by one they used their tails to kill themselves.

I looked up to see Junior with that anxious excited expression he wears during times like this. Randy watched but seemed bored with the whole thing. Mike was looking at the scorpions as if he were mentally writing all this in his head—I guess from a scientific point of view.

The last scorpion seemed to become more frantic as it skittered from side to side, trampling over the already dead scorpions and searching frantically for an escape. It looked like the scorpion might have found one when the fire from one side of the ring started to disappear, but before it could make for safety, Junior grabbed the silver flask from my hand and lit the open end of the circle on fire again, squelching any hope.

It made one last ditch effort to escape and then stood still for a few moments.

I was still fascinated with the experiment. I was amazed that these things could consciously kill themselves when they realized there was no escape.

I believe Kenneth was appalled by it all. His face was pinched as if he hurt and his eyes were squeezed shut. He kept saying, "Holy crap, holy crap!" over and over again.

Finally, the last scorpion stabbed its own head with its tail and ended its life.

Randy saw what Kenneth was doing and walked over to him. He said a few quiet words and then led Kenneth slowly to the tents.

I suddenly felt like it was my fault the little suckers had stuck themselves in the head. Randy knew what we were going to do. Junior looked for a full hour for the scorpions. Just because Kenneth's here now and has some sympathy for little insects doesn't mean that the rules have changed. He makes it out like he and Kenneth are the only ones on this camping trip and everyone else is an evil nuisance spoiling everything.

I got up after the gasoline extinguished itself and walked over to my tent. Glancing over at Mike, I threw him a shrug of my shoulders. He just nodded his head. Mike was like that—he just got things without any words. Mike walked over to the tent he was supposed to share with Junior and laid right in the middle. "Well, Junior—good night."

"No way, I'm not sleeping outside! Don't you hear that storm coming?" Junior wailed. He tried to get a foot in the tent.

"You should think about things like that. You didn't care that the scorpion almost made it out. That's never happened before. You can sleep outside where you can think about the error of your ways," I said to him while I made sure the tent was waterproof. I got that little bit from one of my math teachers at school. She was always saying that *Daniel, you must sit in detention and think about the error of your ways* or *Daniel, you just don't think about the error of your ways.*

She was a hoot sometimes and so very predictable. I would repeat her words sometimes when she wasn't looking. Kids around me always thought that was funny. So did I, which is why I gave her the most trouble. Some teachers are too easy.

Junior gave up trying to get into Mike's tent after about ten minutes. Mike wasn't like me. He was much calmer and didn't really care whether Junior got on his nerves. He had patience. I hadn't really gotten into the story of Mike had I? I know, I said I would.

Mike works for his dad. His dad owns an auto mechanic shop on Main Street. It's a pretty busy street. Well, for a small town like this anyway. It's in a good location and he always has work.

The name of the shop is Big Rick's Auto Repair and he is big. He's a bigger version of Mike. Six foot five, two hundred and sixty-five pounds and missing a right pinkie finger from a dropped transmission. He uses the nub of it to pick his nose from time to time, and it looks like he has it up to his third knuckle, crazy. That really grosses me out. But hey, what's a guy to do with his stump?

I really don't care for him much mostly because of the way he treats Mike. Mike works hard all day and sometimes all night.

One time, Mike fell asleep in school for three days in a row. The teacher got so fed up with having to wake Mike up every few minutes that she called his dad. I don't really blame Mike, Mrs. Wright's classes were pretty boring.

I tried telling her that a few times, but she didn't believe me, even with the proof right in front of her snoring away. She probably thought Mike was on drugs or something. I'm not sure what she hoped to accomplish by calling his father; everyone knows what kind of a jerk he is. But, I don't think she got the response she was looking for.

Mike told me later that his dad gave her a piece of his mind and then hung up on her. Mike didn't show up to school for a few days after that but when he did, it looked like he had been shot at and missed but shit at and hit. His bruised eye, swollen lip, and limping told us all that Mike would never sleep in anyone's class again. Even if his father was responsible for his exhaustion.

His father once had this client that wanted his truck fixed ASAP and would pay extra if it was. Old Rick was only too happy to oblige and beat his sons if they didn't accomplish the work. Forget sleeping when there is work to do.

Luckily, Mike was blessed with patience and is a pretty laid back kind of guy. He didn't mind Junior's whining most of the time. Like I said, he never participated in the things we did to other kids, nor did he participate in our little experiment now that I think about it. I knew, however, that if it did rain on us, Mike would let Junior in.

I looked over to see what Randy and Kenneth were whispering about now. They were still huddled together looking like their talk was so damn important. More important than anything else out here.

I still couldn't believe he was here and taking up Randy's time like that. We didn't even stay up late into the night talking our BS.

Unbelievable.

The quiet of the night here in West Texas is wonderful. There are no sounds except for small insects and the occasional rustle of the wind.

It was calming to be out there. No city rumblings, lights, or cars. Not that Stockton was a metropolis, but you get the picture.

As everyone got quiet and settled in for the night, I could hear some of what Kenneth and Randy were saying. I could hear them pretty clearly now, especially Randy.

I think he may have wanted me to hear their conversation.

"I know he's a little rough, but I think it's all show," Randy said a little louder.

"Well, I knew he wouldn't want me here, but I'm glad that I came. Thanks for inviting me, man. I don't think I could handle another night with my mom crying all night."

"My mom says she's taking it real hard. Mom made dinner for you guys a few times already and sent it over with the church ladies."

"Yeah, it's funny that someone dies and people start sending food. It happened like that with Dad too. Dad died and two hours later the house is full of casseroles. Did you know that grief kinda takes hunger out of you? It like steals it," Kenneth said shifting to get comfortable in his tent.

"Were you close to your brother?" Randy asked.

"Yeah, he wrote to me all the time to tell me what city he was in. He loved the traveling he was able to do. Said he had girls at every port and that Okinawa was the best time he ever had. I never got a chance to ask him what happened there that he liked so much, but I can only imagine. He sent me a letter from Iraq right after he got there and complained so much about the sand. He said it got into everything."

"I bet he liked it though, being able to be out there and seeing things no one in this two-bit town has seen."

"Well, I know he liked it, but was it all worth his life? I don't know. He wasn't like me at all. He was popular. He wasn't a loser; he had a bazillion of friends and the girls were always after him. I think my mom wishes it was me instead of him," Kenneth said a little quieter.

"I don't think—"

"No really, not in a bad way, but I always knew she liked him more. It was just the way it was. I see her look at me now and she kinda looks through me. Not really at me . . . ."

I stopped listening after that. I made myself stop. He was pathetic.

He was feeling sorry for himself. Blaming others like his poor mom on the way he feels about himself. His mom is probably right to feel the way she does.

I can't stand people who feel sorry for themselves all the time. Freakin' pity party!

"I sometimes wish it had been me," Kenneth whispered.

The Bully in ME

At first I thought I imagined it, maybe it was the wind. Something rustling the mesquite trees or the howl of the wind coming up on our perch atop the plateau.

But then I knew. He really felt that desolate.

Well, hell. Everyone has their own shit.

9. The Hershey Squirts

The night brought an abundance of rain. It hadn't gotten into my tent, but everything else was wet. Here in the great West Texas, rain is hard to come by so the terrain looks a lot like a desert with cactus but without the sand. We have rock and lots of it. When it rains, the ground soaks up the water like a greedy sponge. So we didn't need to worry about mud and there were hardly any clouds in sight.

This was a good sign.

This was going to be a good day. I just knew it, and not even Kenneth the wuss was going to ruin this one.

I got up out of my tent, stretched, and glanced around to see who else was up. Mike and Junior were already up and looking for something, "What you gals doing?"

"Junior's not doing well. I think he's got the Hershey squirts," Mike said and smiled at me. "We can't find the t.p."

"Last time I checked that was Junior's job. We bought the little pack. All he had to do was bring it in his backpack," I said laughing now a little bit.

"I don't see how any of this is funny. I really gotta go, and I have to climb all the way down the plateau to use it," Junior barked.

He was now frantically looking for the toilet paper. He was holding onto his stomach with one hand and his butt with the other and he didn't look like he was going to last much longer. Sweat and perspiration started appearing on his upper lip and he looked a little queasy.

Reaching our perch atop the plateau was a big problem when we first approached yesterday, but Mike had found an easier route to go up. That was the only side that was climbable. Well, easily anyway; the other side was a straight drop. The north side of the plateau was less steep. Big leaning boulders crept up the side and it was climbable, but only for the experienced or, at least the fit.

Junior was neither of those; he was not fit, nor was he in any way experienced. The plateau was bare except for a few boulders no bigger than a basketball. There was no place to go to the bathroom up here. He would have to trek down the long way.

I didn't think he could make it. "I bet you five he won't make it all the way down. Bet he'll drop pants half-way there and we'll have to climb around it for the next three days."

Mike smiled a little. "I kinda feel sorry for the kid. Getting the Hershey squirts out here and no toilet paper? That's luck."

"Yeah, going camping with your friends—fifty bucks; a new pair of hiking boots—thirty; getting the Hershey squirts on your camping trip—priceless."

I do have my humorous moments.

Mike laughed a little harder and we enjoyed the moment. Well, until I heard another . . . snort. That would be a good way of describing it. I knew right away it was Kenneth. He must've heard our conversation. I looked over and the pudgy thing was having trouble getting out of the tent.

I looked back over at Mike and then back at Junior who was still holding out while trying to climb down and hold his stomach.

"How about it, five?" I completely ignored the idiot. I

could hear Kenneth fumbling with the zippers on the tent.

"I'll take your offer. I say he makes it all the way," Mike said pointing at Junior. "He already made it halfway."

"Naw, he won't make it. He's already loosened his pants," Randy said, yawning and stretching beside me.

"You in?" I asked.

"No, but I'm going over there to give him some paper towels though. They may be hard and rough, but it's better than nothing. He didn't think of that when he was looking for the paper?"

"Nope." That was all Mike could manage because he was laughing so hard. Junior hadn't made it down all the way. He just stopped and crouched in the middle of two boulders and went at it.

"You owe me five," I said to Mike. I went over to grab some breakfast. I knew some burritos from yesterday were still in my pack. No way was I going to let Junior make something to eat now.

We finished our breakfast quickly and started talking about what we were going to do for the rest of the day. I told them we were going to hunt for a little while and then take a swim in the Pecos River.

No one said otherwise, of course, so we went about the business of preparation. I know it might not seem like much preparation was needed, but we had to discuss a course of action—where we would be headed, who would do the shooting—small things like that.

I told Randy to make sure he gave Kenneth the quick do's and don'ts of hunting. I didn't want him getting in my way. I didn't want to have to go back early if the idiot went and shot himself or, worse, someone else.

We finally made it out of there before noon, which in my humble opinion was pretty good. It left the rest of the day free and clear to do whatever we wanted. We weren't exactly hunting for deer, so there was no reason why we should leave at the buttcrack of dawn. We would be hunting for rabbit or something small like that. I didn't want to have to clean anything too large.

We started out towards the low end of the plateau where it was easiest to climb down. I led the group around and towards the river. My reasoning was this: where there was water, the animals were sure to go and get a drink of it. There aren't many places to go for water here, so it seemed like a sound idea to me.

We got to the river and I gave each of them a station for lookout. They split up and crouched down low to wait.

I tried to get Kenneth and Randy as far away from each other as possible. I figured they would talk through the day and no game in their right mind is going to come near.

They did stay away from each other. Well, for all of thirty minutes or so. I saw Kenneth wave at him and Randy got up to see what he wanted. He probably needed to go to the restroom and couldn't wipe his own ass.

We waited there for what seemed like an eternity, but nothing came near. I was getting angrier by the minute because Kenneth and Junior were now together and they wouldn't shut up. This was all getting frustrating. Junior also had to use the restroom every twenty minutes. Animals can smell human feces from a mile away (I read that somewhere).

With all the talking and the shitting going on, well, it's no wonder we didn't shoot anything. I guess we were having bologna sandwiches again for lunch.

"Alright, there's nothing. Let's take a swim," I said, getting up from my perch and putting the gun aside.

It was a cool rifle, too. My Boss rifle was given to me by my grandfather. He was a crazy old geezer and would say whatever came to his mind. I always thought my grandfather had a genetic defect in the part of the brain that warns you NOT to say something. He had once taken me out on a Sunday for "man talk" and handed me the rifle like it was some kind of ceremony. Excitement couldn't describe what I felt, especially when I looked the gun up on the internet. Turns out it's one of the top ten best rifles to own.

Unfortunately, because of the stupids, I wouldn't be able to use it today. I thought about shooting cans, but crossed that out because I didn't want to waste the ammo.

"Isn't the water cold? Do you think it's safe?" Kenneth whimpered as he looked to Randy for answers.

Are you kidding?

Of course he wasn't. Kenneth took his time getting in the water. I, along with Mike and Junior, jumped right in. It was icy cold but it felt real good.

Randy was too busy with his full-time babysitting job to have any fun. He was trying to coax Kenneth into the water.

Pathetic. I get to a point where I can minimally stand Kenneth, and then he goes and does something like this. At our age, we shouldn't be coaxed into anything, especially something as mundane as getting into the river. I mean, hell, didn't he at least want to take a bath?

"Get in and wash your butt," I ordered finally getting bored with his theatrics.

"Leave him alone Daniel," Randy groaned, not even looking in my direction. I think he was getting a little frustrated, too. It can't be an easy thing to admit when you make a huge mistake. Inviting someone like Kenneth is asking for trouble. He had to know that by now.

"Let the pansy fend for himself." I was getting pretty frustrated now myself. This little piece of crap had already messed up things just by being here. I didn't think I could take anymore of his whining and grunting.

Splashing and laughing, Mike and Junior played in the water like they had no worries. Did they not see what Kenneth was doing to all of us? We couldn't even have fun here in the river, which I knew was one of Randy's favorite things to do. He used to play King of the river. He always wanted to play that game.

But are we?

No.

Because of that pansy we can't do anything. "Wait a

minute. Why don't you just push his ass in? It would save you and me a lot of trouble. It's not like the pansy's gonna drown; the damn water is only about three or four feet deep. Kenneth's as tall as I am and of course pigs float, don't they? All that fat's gotta float!"

Randy rolled his eyes at me then looked at Kenneth. "Don't worry about him. Just put one foot in at a time; hell you don't even have to get in."

That did it.

I couldn't believe Randy was actually putting ME down because of this little twerp. "Can't you just leave him alone? I told you not to let him come."

I got out of the water, mad as heck. "Junior! Mike! Let's go!"

I picked up my clothes and shoes and started walking to camp. I had to go slow because I was too mad to wait for them and didn't want to give them extra time to catch up while I put my shoes on.

We walked in silence for a few minutes when I heard *its* voice again.

"I coulda just got in Randy," Kenneth pouted, trying to appease Randy because it looked like Randy was really mad this time.

"Shut your mouth, Kenneth. You aren't good for nothing. You're useless. I can't figure out how you live everyday," I muttered under clenched teeth.

"Don't talk to me like that. I didn't do anything to you!" Kenneth really felt brave that day.

I stopped walking, turned around, and just looked at him. I was ready to pounce on the idiot, but I knew Randy would probably get in it, so I just stood there. Randy and I shouldn't fight over this idiot. He was definitely not worth it. I dared Kenneth to say something. Of course, he didn't. He took a step back and looked at me warily.

"That's what I thought," I said as I turned and walked back to camp.

Junior murmured something next to me, which I thought was a possible insult, so I yelled at him, "What did you say?"

A little wide-eyed, Junior gestured with his chin. "I said that the plateau looks really high from this point. I bet I could climb that."

He pointed at a steep climb that an experienced climber could probably climb with no problem. Junior, on the other hand, could never climb that thing, even if he worked out all year and it was one of his best days.

No way.

"I think I could do it," Kenneth said.

That stopped me dead in my tracks. I couldn't believe he said that. Was he delusional? Was he out of his mind? I would've laughed at him on any other day, but today I had had enough. I didn't want him here, I didn't want to have to hear his whining for another few days, and I was still angry that he was taking up most of Randy's time.

I took one quick look at Randy, in time to see his look of exasperation. He looked up slowly, and then looked down, shaking his head. I knew, at that moment, Randy was thinking the same thing I was.

The guy couldn't keep his big mouth shut to save his life.

10. The Fall of the Noble

"I'd like to see you climb that wall, then, if you think you can do it," I said to Kenneth. If he was dumb enough to volunteer himself for our amusement, then who was I to deprive the others of this entertainment?

"I could climb it if I wanted to," Kenneth stammered as he looked up at the steep wall.

Sitting down on a boulder near the wall of rocks, I said in a bored voice, "Alright, go ahead. Show us what you got."

I knew he wasn't going to climb that wall. I just wanted to show Randy what a loser he was. Boasting about his abilities, then doing nothing about them, was typical of guys like Kenneth. I wanted Randy to see what I saw. Maybe then we could send him home and we wouldn't have to put up with him anymore. Then, I could enjoy the rest of our camping trip and have fun.

Then again, Randy might find it in his heart for some reason or another to walk the pansy home. I couldn't let Randy go without us because then we'd have to cut things short. Then again, he might fall off and then we'd have to get home. Either way, I think Randy was finally realizing that bringing Kenneth was not the brightest of ideas.

Kenneth was stretching his legs and arms looking up, I guess to plot his path up the boulders. I rolled my eyes and laughed at him. "What are you doing? You and I both know you aren't gonna climb that thing."

"I'm gonna climb it. A couple of years back my mom took me to a carnival. They had a rock wall to climb and I didn't have any problems with that," Kenneth boasted with confidence.

I couldn't help it, I laughed so hard. I had seen several of those at some of the festivals we went to in Odessa. It was a small twelve-foot wall that most of the elementary kids would line up for hours to climb.

This wall in no way, form, or fashion resembled the kiddie climb you find at carnivals. I couldn't believe he was comparing the two. Mike must have been thinking the same thing. "Come on man, you know that's not the same thing. There are no ropes holding on to you here."

"Yeah, but this climb is not steep like the wall I climbed. This one has slants and boulders to climb. It looks easier," Kenneth said now stretching his fingers.

Yeah, fingers. Why he felt he needed to stretch his fingers to climb, I'll never know.

"Don't climb it man. *I* think you can do it. Let's go see what we can cook up to eat. I don't want anymore burritos. Sorry, Daniel but burritos for three days. Well, I want something different," Randy said as he picked up his clothes and started to walk around to the other (safer) side of the plateau.

Finally, the voice of reason. Well, sort of. Randy at least was trying to get him to stop making a fool out of himself.

I looked at Kenneth, smiled, and then got up and gave him the chicken sign by curling my arms and flapping my elbows.

Maybe that's what did it.

Kenneth started to climb and I started to laugh when he slipped on his first step onto one of the boulders. Sheer determination made him take the second step.

Just then, Randy put his hand on Kenneth and forced him onto the ground. "You aren't climbing that thing, let me do it."

"I can do it; let me prove to him that I can," Kenneth said trying to climb back on the boulder.

"You don't have to prove anything. Look, I want to do it."

Randy was trying real hard to save Kenneth's ass. Kenneth looked thankful—and that made me angry. "Why do you have to save him? He's the one that opened his big mouth. He's the one that should have to climb that stupid wall. He's ruining our whole trip!"

Randy started to climb without saying a word to me. I didn't seriously think he would do it, and part of me wanted to tell him not to. I felt that telling him now after the arguing would only set his resolve. He was going to do this now no matter what I said. I knew how Randy thought. He was probably mad at me for starting in on Kenneth. This was his way of getting back at me—proving his point and showing off. It was definitely Randy's style.

One summer when Randy and I were younger, we got this wild notion of joining Boy Scouts and our fearless leader got us all lost, so we ended up at a plateau similar to this one.

At the base of the plateau, there was a wide crevice that came together in the shape of a V. As we got closer, we could see bones of dead animals. It looked like they had either fallen to their death or they just couldn't climb any further and the predators had eaten them. Bones were littered everywhere.

Our pack leader looked worried and decided that he needed to get to higher ground, so he could look over the area to see if he could locate any landmarks. It entered my mind that climbing that wasn't something I wanted to do. I remember thinking that he must be a complete idiot. Even at an early age, I knew I had to take charge.

I also knew that he wouldn't listen to me because I was a kid, so I made up a story about having to take a whiz. To keep track of all of us, he had to keep us together which meant walking to the other side of this crevice to take a whiz. That was all I had to do to distract the numbskull. Little did our pack leader know that Randy and I had been through those parts hundreds of times. We'd go out there searching for arrowheads that my cousin (more on him later) insisted were there. Other times, we'd go out just to get lost. Getting lost was some pretty exciting stuff in the big metropolis of Fort Stockton.

As it turned out, the other side of the boulder was a perfect place to walk—and I mean walk up that plateau. Even back then, we were stronger and faster than the other kids, especially Randy. We were the first ones up. We both died laughing because we weren't more than a hundred yards from our camp site. Our pack leader was such a loser.

So now here we are, years later and it's like a perfect déjà vu. Common sense says we should just go around, but, now, Randy looked as determined as ever. Kenneth said he wanted to make the climb, but he sure didn't resist when Randy stepped around him and began to scale the wall. I could tell Randy was somewhat experienced. I was no rock climber, but I knew it was difficult to get your foot on exactly the right rock to ensure good footing on the next, but he was making it look so easy.

He really was thinking ahead. I could see which way he was heading, and I could tell that the climb would get better once he was over the steeper part. Two large boulders were in his way of success. He was about ten feet up when Kenneth started pleading with him to stop climbing. It looked higher now than it had when we were up there looking down.

Mike was also trying to get him to stop by telling him to quit showing off.

The boulders were not jam packed together but had big gaps between them. This made the climb harder to accomplish because you really had to be careful not to slip into them.

I stepped off to the right and noticed that he was headed toward the steepest part. That's when I felt the first sudden chill creep up my spine. I thought something terrible was about to happen. "Okay Randy, you've proven your point. You can do it and better than any one of us. I don't think we could've gotten that far. Come on down."

I saw him pause for a few seconds then look down at me. He gave me a big smile and lifted one of his eyebrows like he does when he's flirting with a girl he likes. I just knew that he continued to climb because he was enjoying it, not because of what I said. He was obviously getting an adrenaline rush because he started to pick up his pace.

Still.

"Come on, we've gotta cook some dinner. I'm starving," I yelled.

Suddenly, Randy lost his footing and slipped. He was able to hold on for a few seconds, but then he lost his grip. He slid down one boulder and caught himself. He looked back at me and I could tell by the look in his eyes that it had scared him.

"Randy, come on. I really am hungry. I'll cook," I offered in a last ditch effort to get him to come down.

He gave a little laugh, "You don't even know how to cook. Are you gonna cook or you gonna make Junior do it?"

"I'll do it if it makes you come down," I pleaded.

I knew full well that I wouldn't. But if it would get him down then it was well worth the lie.

It happened in the blink of an eye. Randy's arms flailed out like a windmill and his feet reached out in a last ditch effort to cling to the rock. He tried catching himself on the way down, but his head hit the edge of a boulder and just like that—it was over.

He fell to the ground as if in slow motion. He looked like a rag doll falling helplessly, hitting every boulder and cactus bush on his way down. We were all stunned and no one said a word. The sound of his body slamming against the rock was like the snap of an old brittle twig, a very distinct sound that reminds me of fall when the leaves crumble beneath your feet.

I didn't react. I didn't try to catch him. I just watched him fall.

11. Desperation

Randy hadn't fallen all the way down, but was stuck up there halfway down and screaming in agony. His screams were heart-wrenching and scary, but also eye-opening. We all moved to reach him, but we had to make the same climb Randy had just made, so it took what felt like hours to get to him.

Mike and I reached him first. Blood gushed from his head, but the grotesque way his leg was twisted looked like it came out of a sci-fi movie with gruesome special effects. My first thought when I reached him was to reposition his leg.

I could see the bone sticking out and blood was trickling out where it had ripped through his jeans. The scrapes on his face looked shocking, but I knew that was the least of our worries. The back of his head had deep gashes and I could see the inside of his head just above the eye. It was bone.

Randy's screams were deafening now, but Kenneth's scream overpowered Randy's when I reached to touch Randy's leg. You could see the color draining slowly from Randy's face. He went from a golden tan to a mask of white purple agony. It was obvious he was going into shock and with good reason. In all our years as friends, I had never seen him cry, but tears were flowing freely down his face.

"Randy, Randy can you hear me? Are you alright?" Kenneth asked. He looked like he was going to shake him.

"Don't touch him you asshole! Haven't you done enough?" I yelled, pushing him out of the way.

"What are we gonna do?" Junior was pacing back and forth really freaking out. I had never seen him so crazy. He didn't know what to do with himself and just kept looking to me for answers. He didn't get near Randy, as if his injuries were contagious.

"We keep pressure on the wound and one of us has to go for help. Junior, go get me some shirts and water. Kenneth, find two long poles. Junior, make sure you get some rope," Mike ordered. I think that was the first time I had ever really heard Mike make a complete sentence.

Mike was moving around quickly. He looked at me and it seemed like he was a different person. I didn't even recognize him. His face was set in grim determination and he looked very sure of himself and the situation.

"Daniel, you're the most fit. You'll have to go for help. Don't stop until you find someone to come out here."

I could hear him but didn't understand what he was saying to me. I'm sure I was looking at him with a dumb doe-eyed look. I was trying to process his transformation along with Randy's injury, but couldn't seem to snap out of it. I could see myself as if I were looking down at the scene. Junior paced, Mike looked at me and seemed to be saying something in slow motion, and I could see myself staring at him like I was in space. I wasn't aware that I hadn't moved and I hadn't even acknowledged his words or the fact that Randy had stopped screaming and passed out. Kenneth was next to me again with his head bent and he looked to be praying. He was murmuring under his breath praying, "*Please, God.*"

"Daniel! Daniel!" Mike yelled as he shook me hard.

That must have done it. I knew exactly what I had to do.

"I'll help you move him down. You won't be able to do it yourself," I said quickly looking around for some kind of wood to make a pallet. We would have to get him down somehow.

"No, you need to go. I'll get Kenneth and Junior to help me," Mike said pushing me away.

"No, I . . . I need to help," I stammered. I didn't want to leave him. I wanted to stay and make sure he was okay.

"You are his only hope," Mike stated.

I knew he was right and I knew time was critical for him, but I didn't want to leave. I had to, though; I had to run and run fast.

I took one last look at Randy, said a little prayer, and took off. I had seen him trying to open his eyes, but didn't take the time to stop and try to talk to him. I knew time was not on our side. I had to get help fast. I took off and ran as fast as I could. I took nothing with me except what I had on; I didn't prepare, I just left. I didn't even look back. I wasn't thinking about anything but getting help.

As I ran, all I could think about was Randy playing football. I loved to play football with him. He and I were the stars. It was great. He was on offense and I was on defense—a perfect combination that allowed us to let each other know what we did wrong. The girls were crazy for him, too. He was the All-American kid.

His heart was good, too. Sure he went along with me and my bullying career, but he never started any of it. He just fooled around and pestered the dumb nerds. Not as mean as I was, though. His sister was one of his best friends.

My mind would not let me think about what had just happened. My thoughts rumbled through Randy's life and his accomplishments.

Randy would be okay. He would be back on the field next Friday for the homecoming game. He would make a few touchdowns, the girls would be calling him every second, and the unknowing parents will still love him.

Randy always had an amazing way of handling parents. His manners and his All-American looks could settle a doting father's nerves quickly.

We met a very pretty new girl last year, Kandice. She was talked about and looked at by every kid in the school. Randy happened to have a class with her and asked her out. She said she would love to go out with him, but was not allowed to go anywhere because of her overprotective father. Randy just smiled at her and told her to let him take care of it.

I remember looking at him and wondering how he was going to convince her father he wasn't going to try to jump her bones.

Randy took the girl out the following week. Things came too easy for Randy sometimes.

Randy's sister absolutely loved him. They had the kind of relationship that made even me wish I had a sister. She was pretty good about letting us use her car when we asked her to.

A rattle.

I heard it as soon as I came near it. I had been running for a while. I looked behind me to see how far I had gone. I felt like I had walked only a few steps. I could still see the mesa where we had set up camp.

I couldn't believe that I hadn't gotten any farther and I couldn't believe I hadn't let anyone bring their cell phone. How stupid was that? I could've called for help and stayed with Randy.

I turned and picked up the pace. I had to hurry.

Again, I heard the unmistakable jangle of a rattlesnake. I changed my direction enough to try to stay away from it. That would be all I would need.

I could see it now, the headlines would read: Stupid Boy Dies Trying to Save His Best Friend. A little lengthy, but it could happen.

Friend.

Randy was definitely my friend. We had grown up together since kindergarten.

He was someone I could count on. He was the only guy I would never try to bully around.

He had done too much for me. We thought alike on many aspects. He was a great guy.

My steps suddenly quickened. I had to get help. I was no longer important. I had a mission. I started to run as fast as I could.

I was thankful for my little canteen of water. I hadn't taken one drink of it yet. I had just realized that when I saw a car slowing down.

I had somehow reached the highway. A man dressed in tan clothes and a cowboy hat got out of the car. He had a look on his face that seemed strange to me. Like he was seeing ghosts or a long lost relative.

I was the one that was supposed to be frantic. I wanted to yell at him not to look at me like that. I wasn't important, only Randy, but I couldn't even speak when I reached him. I gasped when I tried to say something. Nothing came out of my mouth.

Not a whimper, not a sound. I was wasting time.

He put his arm on my shoulder. "Take it easy son. Let's get you in the car. I'll take you to town and you can call your parents." He was trying to lead me to his car.

I refused to walk to the car and angrily shrugged his hand off my shoulder.

Breathing was difficult as I tried to steady the erratic thumping of my heart. After several agonizing minutes, I finally told him what happened.

The old man wasted no time asking stupid questions. He ran to his truck, grabbed his cell phone, and called the police.

A phone.

Again, I thought about the phone.

Me, in my infinite wisdom, had refused to let anyone bring a cell phone. All because I thought Randy would be on it 24/7 so I had stupidly refused. How could I?

Why would I not bring mine in case of an emergency?

The old man struggled to get me into his truck, but I wouldn't budge. Maybe it was the look of sheer terror and desperation on my face, maybe it was because my clothes were bloodied, or maybe, just maybe, it was because I had somehow, along the way, forgot to put on my shoes. My feet looked like they had been through a grinder.

By the time the Life Flight helicopter reached Randy, it was too late. Randy had bled to death.

12. Full Circle

The funeral was hard. Too hard. Maybe I could've helped him or caught him or tried harder to talk him out of climbing the wall. Maybe, if he had listened to me and left Kenneth in the morning when I got angry, none of this would've happened. We wouldn't be here with all this pain surrounding everything.

I froze at the moment when he fell; I didn't try to help, I just stood there. If I could have somehow broken his fall or moved to get under him, things would have turned out differently.

Maybe, if I had been the one to stay behind I would've been able to be there and help him. I'm smart. I could've done something, but I didn't. Instead I just stood there and ran away. Yeah, I went to get help, but it was for nothing. I did nothing for him. I wasn't even there with him when he died.

Nothing.

It's what I felt inside. I didn't feel that gut-wrenching

pain of losing someone. I didn't feel anything.

It took me a little while to reach the burial site because I wasn't used to the crutches I had to use. Both of my feet were still bandaged up.

The priest began his sermon and we all bowed our heads to pray. I just got angrier and angrier. God taking someone like Kenneth, who was useless and nobody likes anyway, I could understand. Taking Randy? That was ridiculous.

Randy was my friend—probably the only friend I really had.

And now he's gone.

The priest spoke for what seemed like forever about the angels and their need for someone like Randy to be in Heaven with them. All the things the priest said were ridiculous. How can you make such a senseless death sound even remotely reasonable? You need him, God? Well, here he is.

No.

God didn't do this for any logical reason. I was angry at everything. If my mother could have heard my thoughts, she would have had a heart attack. I didn't care though. I didn't care about anything.

After a few minutes, people somberly filed out. They made a slow procession to the coffin and put red or white roses on top. The crying just seemed to get louder. The outcry of this injustice rose as more and more people realized the finality. There was a row of girls Randy had gone out with that were crying too. Randy never really cared about any of the girls but one. They acted like he was something to them. He didn't care about them. It was almost funny.

Almost.

His girlfriend, Yna, was different and had been with him through a lot since seventh grade. They had their ups and downs, but everyone thought they would get married eventually. They were always together. But that was before this.

I looked for her in the crowd, but couldn't see her. She probably couldn't bring herself to come. I scanned the crowd again and caught a glimpse of her standing alone, off to the side. Here eyes were glued to the coffin. Like me, she wouldn't acknowledge anyone.

I wanted to wait until everyone had left. It took three men to pull Randy's father away from the coffin. He yelled, "No!" over and over again and refused to let go. I thought the men would give up after ten minutes, but they kept on trying to make him let go. I wanted to shout at them to leave him alone and let him grieve, but I couldn't say anything. After a while, I didn't want to even look at him. Randy's mother lowered her head and wept in anguish. His sister seemed lost as she quietly rose and walked away.

Desolate and standing alone, I refused to look at my mom when she tugged at my jacket. She murmured something to me, then quietly walked away with Luke.

After everyone left, I limped slowly to the coffin and put my hand on it. It was cold to the touch and had the smell of a new car. A new car?

How ironic.

I ran my hand over the smooth surface wondering how long it would last until it started to decay. Would the worms get to him? Would he realize what was happening to him? Could he see us from where he was? If he was watching, I had the feeling that he was very disappointed; he was probably looking at me and wondering why I wasn't crying. The workers gently moved me back to lift the coffin. I couldn't believe Randy was really in there.

Frozen in place, I watched the workers slowly lower the smooth coffin closer to the cold opening.

"I can't believe he's gone," Yna said suddenly, startling me. I didn't even hear her walk up. I glanced at her but could find nothing to say. What could I say that would help?

Nothing.

I couldn't say shit that would help her or anyone else. I put my head down again and closed my eyes. Still, I felt nothing.

"I keep thinking he's gonna come to my window or call

me on the phone and we'll have a big laugh about all this. I used to think we would get married . . . I always thought we'd have beautiful kids. He would be a coach and I would have a dancing academy."

I knew she was hurting, but I couldn't bring myself to say anything. I watched the workers lift the coffin over the hole.

"I wish he were here. I wish that he would just put his arms around me. I wish I could see him next week at the homecoming game and watch him make another touchdown. He loved playing football with you." She put her arms around herself and swayed.

She looked at me now and I stole a quick glance at her, but remained quiet.

"Why aren't you talking to me? You haven't said anything; you aren't even crying," she accused through her tears. I'm sure she was looking for someone to be angry at. Someone to blame. I didn't mind taking it. It wouldn't make a difference.

She grabbed my shirt after a while and shook my arm. "Say something! Aren't you going to say something? Do you really have no heart? I know about all those kids you hurt at school. I hear about all the things you've done. You're a horrible person!"

I shook my arm until she let go and calmly limped away. I didn't want to be there anymore to listen to her shit.

I felt nothing.

Absolutely nothing.

Part II
Now

13. Emptiness

My mom wants to take some food over to Randy's house. I remember Kenneth's words from camping about his brother. I can't imagine Randy's family wanting to eat right now. I tried telling Mom about this, but she doesn't seem to understand. To her food is comfort, to me it is a nuisance. I don't think the family wants anyone around.

I refuse to go. I quietly walk to my room and shut the door. I don't want to talk to anyone and I don't want to relive what happened. I don't owe anyone an explanation.

I know eventually that I'll have to return to school and the thought of that kills me. People are going to be looking at me, maybe they'll be thinking that I'm some wierdo or worse—they're gonna feel sorry for me.

The images of Randy lying on a sharp boulder with a broken bone sticking out of his leg don't want to go away. I see myself again crouched down next to Randy's body doing absolutely nothing.

As I wallow in the privacy of my room, I notice my closet door is open. I know I had closed it before I left. Slowly, I walk toward the door, examining my surroundings for any kind of clues left behind by the intruder. Maybe Luke has finally come into my room. I have a mirror in my room behind the closet door. I fully expect to find someone lurking behind the door.

I don't.

I see Randy watching me in the mirror. I jerk my body around, hoping I imagined it all.

But he stands in my room looking grotesque with his leg twisted and his brain slowly seeping out of his head. He watches me and keeps mouthing something, but I can't understand him. I shake my head hoping he will disappear but, he gets closer every time I close my eyes.

"You did nothing," he finally yells, so loud it reverberates against the walls.

Startled and sweaty, I gasp for air as I sit up in my bed.

I must have been asleep for a little while because when I look out the window, it's dark. Thunder roars in the distance; maybe that's what woke me up. I blink a few times, trying to look around and trying to calm my speeding heart. The images of Randy in my room are too real.

Having Randy here again is something I keep hoping for. This is all a bad dream; I'll wake up and it'll be time to go on our camping trip. I would do things differently.

I get up from the sofa in my room and turn on the television. I want to watch a movie and try to get my mind on something else.

Flipping through the channels, I find nothing. I've seen several of the movies but nothing interests me. I turn the television back off and lay down on my bed again.

The telephone rings. I don't bother to get up. I have nothing to say to anyone. My mother must have answered it because I can hear her footsteps coming closer to the door. She doesn't open it but just knocks lightly.

I don't answer.

She knocks again and whispers, "*Mijo*, Kenneth is calling again. Do you want to talk to him?"

I still don't answer. The thought of that idiot calling me

again just pisses me off. What is he doing calling me? Does he not realize that we aren't friends and in no way am I going to take Randy's place as his protector? That's probably what he wants. The idiot.

Mom asks again and I make up my mind. I'll talk to the pansy and tell him to stop calling me.

"Give me the phone Mom," I reply and open the door just enough for her to hand me the phone.

"Dinner is waiting *Mijo*, I made your fav—"

I close the door before she finishes. I don't want to eat now.

I take a deep breath and answer the phone. "What the hell do you want? Don't call me, we aren't friends!"

Calmly, as if knowing my reaction, Kenneth says, "I have a message from Randy."

14. Message from the Dead

No matter how much I tried, he would not tell me over the phone.

He said it was too important and we had some things to talk about first. I can't imagine what the hell we have to talk about and at first, I refused but the asshole just said okay and was about to hang up.

I couldn't let him. Regardless of all the hateful feelings I have toward Kenneth, I still want to hear what Randy had said.

So, here I am waiting outside of the idiot's house. I'm hesitating. I'm not too sure whether I want to get out of the car or stay and wait for him.

When I see Kenneth move a curtain to look through the window, I think he may come and talk outside, so I decide to wait in the car.

Fifteen minutes pass and he still hasn't emerged. Obviously, he isn't coming to me and he isn't making this easy.

If I go to the door and ask Kenneth what Randy said, I'll feel like I'm begging. I sure don't want any favors from this idiot. What could Randy have told this guy that he didn't or couldn't tell Junior or Mike? I don't want to go in there; everything in me wants to knock on that door and start pounding on the pansy, to force him to tell me what Randy told him.

But there is a small part of me—a very small part of me—that doesn't want to know what Randy had to say. Did he blame me for the fall? Did he have some cryptic message of doom that was supposed to be my destiny because I made them all go out on that plateau?

I just want to know what he said without really knowing what he said. Makes no sense, I know, but I just want this to be over with without going through it. Maybe he wants to tell me that there really isn't a message and Kenneth is just looking for an excuse to talk to me.

I will beat the living shit out of Kenneth if he says that. He better make up something, anything.

I sigh as loud as possible and reluctantly open the car door. As soon as I put my foot on the graveled driveway, the front door opens and he sticks his head out. He has obviously been waiting for me to come out the entire time, "Come on in," he says. "My mom made us some cookies."

Jesus, is he serious? Does he really think I came over for a chat and some cookies? Sure, we'll sit in the parlor and drink milk and eat cookies and talk about the weather and the new golf clubs he's purchased.

He is an idiot. Proof right here.

It takes me a few seconds to pull the crutches out of the front passenger seat. Getting up the few steps to his yellow house proves to be a little tricky, since I' not doing any practicing on the crutches. I still can't use them as well as I would like.

It's a typical nerd house: a white picket fence, self manicured shabby landscape, and the all-important Welcome mat on the porch. Sadly enough, this reminds me of his brother who will never be welcomed home.

Entering the house, the unmistakable smell of cinnamon and blueberry candles overpowers my senses. A strange mix.

The living room is cluttered with crocheted blankets strewn over every piece of furniture. Kenneth motions for me to follow him into the kitchen.

His mother stands in the middle of the kitchen with a plate of cookies . . . or something that looks like cookies. They look like clusters of something covered in white sugar. My stomach growls unintentionally. Her smile makes her look even younger. She's a surprise because she looks so much younger now than she did at the funeral. I had never really noticed her before, but now with her yellow cream dress, light brown flowing hair and soft apron, she looks warm and soothing. What the hell am I thinking?

I look down and force myself to concentrate on a glare directed solely at Kenneth. He's perched at the stool, offers me some cookies, and points to a barstool. I keep standing. I am not going to stay long.

"So Daniel, I hear you're a pretty good football player. Kenneth plays football, but I don't like to watch. It's all too scary. You guys have homecoming coming up. Are you still going to play in the game?" Kenneth's mother asks me.

"I'm not sure, ma'am," I say for the utter lack of something else to say. I can't think of that yet.

"You can call me Linda," she says as she places three cookies and something that looks like cottage milk in front of me.

I steal another glance at Kenneth who doesn't bother to look at me, then turn to his mom. She's smiling at me as if she knows I really don't want to be in her house eating cookies with her son. She pushes a stool toward me and patiently waits for me to sit.

With a little sigh, I sit down, promising myself that I'm not going to stay long and this better be worth it. I'm not going to eat or drink any of this, no matter how much his mom smiles at me.

"I'll leave you boys alone for a chat, huh?" she says, leaving the kitchen.

We sit there in silence for a few minutes. Me, sitting there slumped over and glaring outside and him enjoying the hell, it seems, out of those cookies and the turd milk he keeps drinking. I look down at my plate, pick up the glass of whatever is in it and take a whiff. Surprisingly, it smells like chocolate and cinnamon but it's white. I chance a drink and my eyes grow big. It's really good, even though I have no idea what it is. I decide to take a huge bite out of the clusters on my plate and again, I'm surprised that they too are delicious. Finishing my plate in a few bites, I swallow down the rest of my drink. I find myself sitting with a smile on my face . . . .

Here.

What am I doing?

Did I lose my mind? I'm sitting here eating cookies and milk with the fat pansy. I glare at him as I set my drink down. He seems to sense when I lose the awe of my palate.

"So, tell me what he said," I murmur. I refuse to waste anymore time.

Kenneth doesn't say anything for a few minutes but, I'm not going to ask again. "I just wanted to tell you in person what he said. I know you didn't want to come over and I know we don't really like each other, but I made a promise and I have to keep it," he finally says, standing up next to the table with the plate of cookies. At first, I think he's getting more to eat, but instead he picks it up and shoves it in the microwave.

"I just came over so you could tell me what he said. What message did he give you that he couldn't give Mike or Junior, or me?"

"Is that what's bothering you? He told me and not someone else that was there?" He sighs and stares at me. "You make this difficult for me. You've always made things hard for me. You make it hard to like you."

"I don't want you to like me, I don't want to be here and I don't want to be friends. Take that out of your silly, pathetic mind," I yell, standing up. I can't believe I've been suckered into coming over here. I can tell he is trying to get to me somehow. I just don't know what he wants from me.

No wait.

Now I got it. He wants to be my friend. He wants me to somehow erase all the trouble he has at school and he wants me to apologize for all that he says I've done to him. Sure, I gave him a hard time a few times at the lockers or in the hallway, but in no way did I ever ruin him. I never stuffed him in the toilet. Not that I can remember anyway. I don't think I ever even beat him up for money. I should have though. Looking at him now, I think I could've really gotten some money out of him. He's such a wuss.

"I don't care if we're friends after this. Like I said, I'm only doing what I promised to do."

"Then why don't you stop fartin' around and tell me what he said?" I'm really getting angry. Part of me doesn't want to know, but this idiot is making it hard for me to stay.

"All right, but before you start interrupting me with questions, just listen until I'm finished," he says taking his seat again and looking out the window.

I don't bother to say anything because I don't trust myself. His remark has really pissed me off, but control is something I pride myself on. I will get back at him one day soon, but for now I just sit back and look out the window too.

"When you took off, he regained consciousness for a few minutes before he went out again. We were all really scared and I didn't know what to do. Mike seemed to know everything and I trusted him and obeyed his orders. He told me to sit with Randy and just keep talking to him. Mike went to look for something to use to stop the blood from trickling out of his wound because it was obvious to both of us that Junior was out of it and not listening to him."

He runs his fingers through his mop of hair, and, after a few quiet moments, continues desperately, "I tried to put my hand over the part of his leg that was bleeding, but it just kept escaping between my fingers. It was like trying to stop a faucet with just your hand; I couldn't do it. His head bled too. Junior was just pacing back and forth talking to himself and he was no use. I even tried putting my shirt on his wound above his eye but nothing I did was working. He kept bleeding, Mike came back and tied something around Randy's leg, but even that didn't help. So Mike said he had an idea. He said he would be right back and just to keep talking to him and keep him conscious."

"Just tell me what I'm supposed to know." I don't want to hear any of this, but Kenneth ignores me and keeps jumbling his thoughts together. It's as if he's trying to get it all out in one sentence.

"I talked about my mom's cooking, my classes at school and my brother—anything I could think of that would help. I rambled on for what seemed to me like hours, but I'm pretty sure now that it must've been only a few minutes. That's when he came to again. I was so glad that he had woken up and I thought this meant that he would be okay. He looked at me with a glassy look and started talking to me about you, his sister, and his girlfriend Yna. He wanted me to tell them something for him and I tried to stop him because I wanted him to tell them himself, but he told me to promise to do this in person. He warned me that you wouldn't want to talk to me but I had to make you. He said I had to tell you that it wasn't your fault, that he climbed that wall on his own and that you were the best friend he ever had—"

At this point I get up and start to walk to the door. I don't feel any better, but at least I know what he wants me to know.

I get it.

It wasn't my fault. This is something Kenneth could've told me on the phone.

"I'm not done," he says still looking out the window. This makes me stop in my tracks, but I don't look at him. I just put my head down and wait for whatever else the idiot is trying to tell me.

"He said that he didn't want you to stop taking your camping trips."

Startled, I steal a glance at him with, I'm sure, my mouth open.

"He wants you to keep going next year and the year after that. Worst of all, he wanted me to tell you to take us all with you, even me. He said you had to make the promise at his grave and stick to it," he yells at me right before I slam the door and take off.

15. Back to Reality

There are so many thoughts buzzing in my head. I try hard to tear apart Randy's words so they make some kind of sense, but I can't. Why would Randy want me to promise something like that and why would Randy ask him to tell me in person? He knew I hated Kenneth.

I can't see myself going back and camping at that place, ever. There's nothing there for me. The bitter memories will be too much, and I certainly can't see myself taking fat boy.

I know eventually I have to go back to school. Luckily, I won't have to go back with those stupid crutches. I ditched them as soon as I had the chance.

I've been delaying the inevitable for the last few weeks, and I'm hoping to get out of it again.

Not a chance.

My father calls me out of the self-induced seclusion of my room. It takes a lot to get me out. First, they send my brother . . . three times.

Then mom comes in and tries the—*Your dad's going to get mad, Mijo*—bit, but I don't move. What can he do? Ground me to my room? Take away the television—which I haven't turned on in days anyway?

I know. He can ground me for a few weeks.

"Get out son, and unlock this door," my father quietly says from the other side of the door. I get up and quickly stumble over a few weeks of clothes. I open the door enough to peek through.

What a bully, huh?

I look at him for a second to evaluate if he's angry, irritated, or just plain hopping pissed. He isn't any of those things. I can always tell.

So, I sigh as loud as I can and walk slowly to the bed to indulge in my self-pity again, but what he says next makes me stop and look at him.

"You will go to school tomorrow. No questions, no excuses and I don't want to hear from your mother that you didn't go or you woke up late. Enough is enough. Get your mind out of your butt and pick yourself up again. You are strong. Show me how strong you can really be."

He doesn't say anything else for a long while, just stares at me as if he wants to say something else or worse come over and hug me. I turn around and throw myself on the bed, "Yes, sir."

That's all I say and he quietly walks away and shuts the door. I don't want to go face all of the questions. I'm not scared of the people or what they will say, I just don't want to hear them talking. Part of me doesn't trust myself and I know I'm angry at everyone anyway. Going to school is only going to make things worse, not better.

I can see myself wanting to go and beat up on those guys that so far have had a nice, lovely week off from me. Maybe I can go to school and get back into the swing of things.

I decide that I'm ready to go to school—not that I really have a choice or anything, but I can see myself going and things being at least tolerable.

I lie down on my bed shortly afterward in the dark and I think of my brother who's pretty much left me alone. I can't remember when I saw him last. I heard him a few times knocking on my door when he was sent by Mom, so I know he's alive. I figure he probably wants the old me back too.

It is time.

* * *

Screaming of battlefields and love, the alarm clock blazes through my hazy nightmare. Randy visits me nightly in my dreams. I can't shake him.

I don't want to get out of bed. The smell of tortillas wafts through the house like a warm, reassuring blanket causing me to dig deeper into the bed. My father's face and his stern warning from last night make me reluctantly get up after a few minutes.

I dress quickly in my favorite blue jeans and long-sleeve green t-shirt before walking into the kitchen.

There are piles of tortillas and burritos in the cooler on the floor. My mom takes one look at me and sighs; I'm not sure if she thinks I look like shit or if she just feels pity. "Oh, *Mijo*. Here, have some breakfast." She hands me two burritos and right away I recognize it as pity. She never allows us to take more than one burrito. They are for selling not for eating, so she likes to say.

But today, I don't have the appetite. I know if I don't take the burritos she will definitely know that something is wrong with me. I have been avoiding this moment for some time, and I am not anxious to get going, but the alternative is Mom and her looks of pity. I choose to go to school early. Maybe I'll just take a drive.

I scoop up the burritos and head for the door before she can look at me with that look again. My father sometimes gets a ride to work with one of his friends so as to leave his green hoopty. Riding with Randy in the mornings is obviously out of the question now, so I guess my dad knows that.

The hoopty's a two-toned green four-door Buick that has definitely seen better days, but it gets me where I need to go and it hasn't let me down yet.

Randy and I used to ride to school together every day, and either he would pick me up when I didn't have the car, or I would pick him up. It was something we did all the time without thinking, so when I turn onto his street, I'm not really surprised. His house has flowers, wreaths and candles on the front lawn. Lots of cars still litter the driveway.

I just keep on going down the street and turn onto Main Street to go for a ride. I'm early and don't want to get to school too early. I drive through town and realize that during my short absence nothing has changed. Everything's still the same. There are no new stores up in town, no tribute to Randy, no change. Nothing.

I decide that maybe going in early is not such a bad idea. I can get parking close to the school, make my way to class and wait in class instead of walking in with the rest of the herd and having to listen to the whispers and see the stares of pity. I don't want to do that either.

Only the nerds and the dumb-asses get to school early enough to get the first row of parking. Randy and I always parked in the sixth or seventh row because we liked just barely making it to class. The nerds came in to brown-nose the teachers and the dumb-assess go to tutorials or detentions because they can't get their heads out their butts long enough to learn anything.

I don't fall into either of these categories, but (at this point) I don't care much what people think.

The front row is, of course, empty, so I park in the closest one and head to my class. As soon as I walk into the school, the smell hits me like a ton of bricks. It seems like every school has this smell to it. Maybe teachers invented the smell years ago and loved the aroma so much that one teacher somewhere in no-mans-land is getting rich off the rights to produce this eau-de-toilet.

Nothing has changed.

The same posters and signs are up on the walls, the same

announcements are present outside of the front office, and the teachers all look the same. None of the teachers try to stop me when they see me walking in before the bell. I guess they aren't going to ask me if I have a pass, so I head to my locker and look over at Randy's locker wondering what the girls have done to it.

Sure enough, they decorated it with bows and flowers. Seriously, Randy was a man not some pansy who would've enjoyed the pinks, pastels and daisies on his locker. I notice that some people have also written things on a banner, so I shut my locker and walk slowly toward his locker to get a closer look.

I'll always miss you and We *will never forget* banners are displayed in bright, lively colors. They were made by some of the girls on the varsity cheerleading team. Most of those girls never even knew him nor did they even care a lick about him. Most weren't lucky enough to have even talked to him.

I'm shaking my head in awe when Mr. Nelson comes over and puts his hand on my shoulder. I don't want him to tell me anything; I know he's gonna start trying to console me or to ask me how I'm doing or something stupid like that.

To my surprise, he doesn't say anything. He quietly stands beside me and stares at it all.

"He didn't even know these people," he says.

This surprises me because it's exactly what I'm thinking. These people are writing things on his locker, yet they didn't even know him. Maybe they were writing on it to make it *look* like he knew who they were. He isn't here anymore to say anything, so they can just make things up.

"He wouldn't be caught dead talking to some of these people." The urge to rip the banners and the stupid flowers to shreds is almost overwhelming. I walk away from it knowing that if I don't I will do just that.

Mr. Nelson doesn't try to stop me, but I can feel his eyes boring down on me as I walk away. Let him think whatever he wants, he isn't any different. He didn't know Randy either.

I arrive in Mr. Farts class; well it's Mr. Farks, but hey if you have a name like that and *you choose to be a teacher and you look like a nerd*—that's what you get.

No one sits in the classroom, not even the esteemed Mr. Farts, so I walk to my usual seat by the door and get my things out. My watch reads five full minutes before the bell rings. I've never been this early and I contemplate whether or not I should hang out in the restroom for awhile, but I don't feel like beating anyone up yet, so that is out of the question. To save my rep I'll have to do something to someone. What am I going to do, just stand there and watch people take a whiz? So I decide this seat is the best place to be.

Mr. Farts walks in and I can see by the startled look on his skinny, glassy-eyed face that he is very surprised to see me here in his classroom. His steps halt just enough for me to know he notices me and then he walks quickly to his desk. I know right then he's looking for something brilliant to say to me and trying to figure out what he can say that won't make him sound like a complete ass. "How are you Daniel?"

Is that the best he can do? For that, I say the one word he's gonna get out of me, "Fine."

Nodding his head as if that word had so many different implications, he adjusts his glasses and tries again for brilliance, "Have you been OK?"

"Fine," I say and again start to go through my binder and look for some imaginary paper I just misplaced. The bell rings and he steps outside; I know exactly where he's headed. He's gonna go see the counselor, a plump middle-aged lonely woman who sits in her office giving useless advice to poor unsuspecting teenage girls that have no one to talk to. The ones that do go talk to her realize quickly that she's even more useless than any of the other people in their lives.

I unwillingly visited her once two years ago when I stuck a kid's face in the toilet. Junior was actually responsible for that one, but no one was gonna believe that, so I was the obvious choice. Her office was full of cat pictures; no, not just different cats but the same cat over and over again. The smells were as stifling as her presence. I spent the next twenty minutes listening to her put her one psychology class to use on me. She spoke of insecurities and attitudes that were present in my life. I had already read something like that in one of my books, so I made the appropriate comments just to make her feel better.

Because of my comments, she mistakenly assumed that I agreed with her. It never occurred to the fat little cat lover that I was making fun of her.

Students begin ambling into the classroom and some daringly sneak a peek at me. I lower my head and pretend to sift through my binder again. I don't want to talk to anyone, and I don't want to hear them say Randy's name. I think they get the picture because I'm pretty much left alone.

As I predicted, a few minutes after the tardy bell rings, the plump little counselor peeks her head in. "Daniel? Can I see you for a minute?"

As if I have a real choice? Maybe I could say, "No, you can't see me for a minute because you're a useless specimen and a free-loading oxygen breather." I don't think that would go over too well.

Of course, I slowly nod my head and get up. All eyes turn in my direction and a few looks of pity float my way from some of the girls.

Outside the classroom, she asks me to follow her. I roll my eyes at her back and proceed to follow her to her stinky office. I can see it now: pictures of the same cat everywhere and the smell of strong candle wax suffocating the air.

As soon as we step in to her room, I notice those horrible familiar scents, but there is another different yet distinct smell—Ben Gay.

Great.

I saunter into her office and notice Mike already slumped in a chair. I throw myself into the seat next to Mike with a little too much force. The old chair strikes the wall but I'm not about to apologize. I give Mike a questioning nod and he shrugs his shoulders as if to tell me—Who *the hell knows?*

While we're waiting for the counselor to stop jabbing her jaw with some other poor unfortunate student, I glance over at Mike. He looks like he hasn't slept in days, his clothes are wrinkled, and he smells like wet dog. When I take a good look at his face I see several bruises, some old and some new. I know it has to be his dad and he'd gone to town on him again.

Like I said, his dad makes a great deal of money off the backs of his sons. Mike is the oldest one so I figure he takes care of the others because they don't have nearly as many bruises on a regular basis like Mike does.

CPS sucks. Ask Mike.

"Hey, Mike, you doing okay?" I ask him. He looks over at me and gives me the same response I gave Mr. Farts earlier. "Fine."

The counselor jingles her way in to the office. She has to move a few things out of the way so she can get to her chair. The earrings she wears clink every time she takes a step and it seems like she intentionally moves her head around to make them rattle more. I guess she's proud of those cheap 99 cent bargain basement earrings.

"I know you're both wondering why I brought you in here," she says finally taking her seat and propping up her nameplate that reads Ms. Hinho (more on that name later). "It's about the incident."

No shit.

Mike and I look at each other and in that instant I know we aren't answering any of her stupid questions. We turn to her and I give her my best blank deer-caught-in-the-headlights stare I can conjure up.

"I know you don't want to talk about the incident, but you have to remember that talking about hurtful things helps to alleviate those ugly little memories I'm sure you both have. Remember that others have come in here to talk to me and I know they feel better after they leave. So, Mike," she turns to him, "why don't we start with you? Can you tell me what you were doing when the incident occurred?" She raises her two hands and curls her two forefingers every time she said "the incident."

When the "incident" occurred? Are we in a CSI movie or something, some investigation? Mike, of course, says absolutely nothing.

She sighs and tries a different approach, "Your teachers have expressed their concern about you, Mike. They've all said the same things: you're not paying attention, you're falling asleep, you're talking back to the teachers, and your grades have dropped so low, you are now failing every class."

The sleeping in class and not paying attention bit is nothing new, but I am startled to hear about the failing grades. Mike is not an outspoken student; he's well liked by all the teachers, he's polite and his grades are always good when his father allows him to come to school. I look over at Mike again and this time I see what I have been missing. His eyes are sunken in and his hands had begun shaking the moment the short piggy mentioned "the incident."

He's grieving for Randy too. I never thought about Mike in that sense. I've only thought about the other idiots that say they know Randy but never did. Mike really knew Randy. Maybe not like I did, but in his own way.

They often went running together; it was the only time they hung out without me and Junior. Randy liked to go with him because he could keep up and it would prepare him for football. I never was sure why Mike ran because he wasn't in any athletic competitions at school, nor did he ever make mention of any aspirations to be. From what Randy said that was a sad thing because he was really pretty good.

"And Daniel," says the corpulent counselor with a sway of her fat finger, "well this is the first time you show up at school since the little incident occurred, and I thought I'd bring you both in together so that we can have a group discussion."

At this point, she puts her chubby little hands together under her fat chin and smiles, "Now, I know you've both been hurt and I want you to think of me as one of your best friends and not like the professional that I am," she says, picking up a pen and notepad. The woman is clearly in the wrong profession. She should seriously look into the CSI show. She can be a stout psychopathic degenerate that taunts and torments the students until one day she unceremoniously brings an AK-47 and shoots at will from the rooftop.

"Now, let's see what level of trauma you guys are experiencing." Clearly, she's going back to her ancient days in college or perhaps some seminar she attended over the summer. I know from some reading I did a few summers ago that victims of bullies go through different levels of trauma. The last levels include suicidal, delirious, and, best of all, homicidal. I'd be willing to bet that the levels she's speaking of are the same. I don't think, however, that in any classes or seminars the instructors advise you to let your victims know they're being evaluated. I think I'll be on level three today.

"Clearly, Mike, according to your teachers, you have exhibited level one behavior, but I think you may be on level two. Can you answer a few questions for me?"

I look over at Mike and notice that he's playing with his fingernails, a habit Randy often had but one I have never seen on Mike. "Have you acted irrationally in the classroom since the incident?"

Again, clearly she is in the wrong profession. If he were irrational, then how would he know it?

"Has your behavior in the classroom changed drastically in the last few weeks?" she asks, still scribbling ferociously on her new yellow pad.

"Have you noticed a sudden drop in communications with the outside world?"

Are you kidding me?

She hasn't even looked up to check if he's heard her or even to hear his answers. With a quizzical look, Mike glances over at me to see if I can believe what we are hearing.

I simply nod my head. What the hell else can I do?

"Now, I think we've established that Mike is on level two

and needs some serious help from myself and my colleagues."
She has colleagues?

She finally looks up from her writing and focuses on poor Mike with a smile that only accentuates her fat cheeks. "We have a very fortunate small group that meets here at the school on Friday nights. It's very informative and loads of fun. Mrs. Jose makes the best popcorn. I truly believe you would benefit from our sessions. Please think about this and I will call you back in next week to make sure you will be joining us. You can go now and I do hope you feel a little better. This talk, I'm sure, has been great for you. I will give you a pass to go back to class."

She squints her beady little eyes at him, hands him a note, and nods her head as if to say—*I know what you've been through and now you and I have a little secret.*

Throwing one final look of pity toward me, Mike practically falls over himself trying desperately to get out of here before she changes her mind. He'd said one word the entire time he had been in the office.

Typical Mike.

"Now," she says, turning toward me and taking a seat again. With a long drawn out sigh, she continues, "I know that beneath that thick, not caring attitude of yours, you are really hurting inside. I know you're a wonderful sweet young man deep deep down inside. We just have to work out a way to make that great considerate young man come out."

She straightens up in her seat, and with a swish of her pen, she starts the same line of questioning she had with Mike. "Have you had any suicidal thoughts? Have you felt an overwhelming urge to harm another person? Do you hear any voices in your head or have you seen things that maybe didn't really happen?"

She doesn't wait for me to answer but continues on with her litany.

"I know you hurt people all the time, and I know that because of that, you feel sorry for yourself and daily or weekly contemplate suicide. I also think you may be hearing things or seeing unreal situations."

Now at this point I just sigh, shift in my seat, and nod my head. If I had suicidal thoughts, how would she know? And seriously, if I saw something happen with my own eyes, how can I tell her if it was real or unreal? She's been reading too many counseling journals or how-to books.

She puts her glasses down and rubs her pudgy little nose. "Look, I feel like you are in a stage three traumatic state. I don't think a simple meeting here with me and my colleagues will suffice. We're good—but not good enough to help a level three student."

I kind of snort, which she obviously doesn't like.

"I was hoping you would be as cooperative as Mike was, but it looks like your attitude is a direct result of your condition. You can go back to class now, but you and your parents will be hearing from a professional at the hospital. I think they'll be able to better serve you."

She grabs a pen, tears off a paper, shakes her head to hear the jingles, and writes me a note to go back to class.

Ironically, I was just like Mike. I didn't say a word.

16. Leave Me Alone

It's been two weeks since I'd gone back to school. I decided not to attend the homecoming football game.

The long talk I had with the coach did nothing to convince me to play in any more games. It won't be the same and I don't see myself wanting to dress-out or workout. My dad didn't even question that one, so that's fine by me.

I haven't had any run-ins with the counselor, nor have I locked a kid in a gym locker. I haven't even been to the restroom except in athletics. I've done absolutely nothing to anyone since I have come back.

Well, to be fair, I did try beating someone up in the restroom at the beginning of school a few days ago.

Mark happened to go in to the restroom right after me. I saw him hesitate, shrug, and step inside. I guess since I hadn't done anything to him since the accident, he felt safe. I pushed him around a little, got five bucks from him, and then, abruptly—I let him go. I thought beating him up would make me feel normal (whatever that means) but it just made me feel hollow and empty afterwards.

It seems like my heart isn't in it anymore. I don't want to look at anyone. I want my old life back, but I can't sleep or beat anyone up.

Yna tries talking to me every day since I came back to school. Ignoring her and walking away is getting harder and harder to do. I don't know what she wants; she just keeps telling me she needs to talk to me. What could she and I possibly have to talk about? I wasn't there at the end with Randy, so I have nothing for her.

I don't want to answer any stupid questions nor do I want to relive what happened. If she has any questions she can go ask Randy's family. Looking at her just makes me feel sick.

Yesterday, she actually came to my house. She talked to my mom for a few minutes, and then quietly tried my door.

I haven't bothered to talk to Junior or Mike or any of my other less important friends. Why would I talk to her? I don't want them near me. Randy can't be replaced so why bother?

Junior has come by the house several times, but I refused to open my bedroom door to let him in. I don't care about how he feels, why should I? He came by the house again a few nights ago and knocked on my window. I opened the window, threw my Coke at him, and slammed the window shut. I don't know what he said or how long he stood out there afterwards and I don't really care.

Junior comes by the house like clockwork. I hear his footsteps nearing my door, and I hold my breath like he can hear my breathing. He knocks on the door, waits several minutes, and then knocks on the door again.

Finally after about ten minutes, Junior leaves without a word. Always the same. I get up from my bed and go to the kitchen to find something to eat. The small fridge in my room is bare for the first time since I got it. Lately, I've been eating not really because I'm hungry, but because I don't want Dad or Mom to look at me with pity or start worrying again.

My mom is in the kitchen as usual, cooking dinner when I walk in.

"*Mijo*, when are you going to talk to your friends? They've been coming over here every day for several weeks, and you don't even talk to them. Junior didn't look good last time I saw him." She can't help looking at me with those sad eyes, but I'm not going to give in. Not on this.

"Mom, he'll stop coming over eventually," I say, grabbing a hot tortilla from the pile. I open the fridge and reach for the butter when she slaps my hand.

"I don't think you give him enough credit. You're going to spoil your dinner," she says, wiping her wet hands on her apron.

"Mom, I can eat ten of these and still eat more than my share of dinner." This isn't entirely true anymore. Most times I get a full plate so as not to get them watching me, but I wasn't eating any of it.

"You're losing weight and I can tell. You don't eat and it's like you're a dead man walking around."

When she mentions the word dead, I flinch inside.

Dead.

Where did that word come from? Who made it up? It's so final. Where do people get the strength?

"Mom, I'm fine. I'm just not working out yet. We're still in off-season. We'll start working out soon and then you'll see me pig out again."

I give her my most brilliant smile and walk quickly back to my room. I certainly don't want her finding out about me quitting football. She never went to any of my games anyway.

I turn on the television and flip through the channels hoping to find some kind of escape from my life. Most things on television are ridiculous. We have over 100 channels of crap. Nothing is ever on and nothing's worth seeing. Reality shows are okay, but you get to a point where it just becomes stupid.

Finally, I find a show on how things work. Boring yes, but it's the best I can do.

Way into my second show, Mom knocks on my door, "*Mijo*, Junior's mother is on the phone. You better answer it."

I certainly don't want to talk to her. "Just take a message, Mom. I'm busy doing my homework." That should work, it usually does. My mother doesn't have a clue what goes on with my school work. She never had to worry about it before, so she's very trusting.

"No, *Mijo*. I won't this time. She sounds really upset and they can't find Junior. She hasn't seen him since yesterday."

"Didn't you tell her that he just left? He was here a few hours ago." I find myself getting frustrated. Why can't people just leave me alone?

"He didn't come over today. A little boy named Kenny came by today." That's my mom. Kenneth is far from little; he's a colossal of a man, okay boy. But in her eyes he's little because he's young.

That's a surprise to me. I thought Junior had come by earlier, not Kenneth. Why would Kenneth come over? There was no need for him to come by. The camping trip wasn't supposed to take place for another year—if we even keep that promise. He probably missed me giving him a hard time. Whatever the reason, he had made me wonder. He probably did that on purpose too.

"I'm coming Mom. I'll get it in a few minutes." Maybe if I take my time she'll hang up. I'm not Junior's keeper. How would I know where he is? I haven't talked to him since I left to find help. I haven't talked to anyone.

"No, *Mijo*. You will not hide from this. You get up right now and answer this phone. This woman needs you. You get up!" I have to admit I've never heard my mother get that tone with me. Whatever this woman told her must have made an impact. The knocking on my door is getting louder. That's all I need for her to do—tell dad.

I get up quickly, open the door, and snatch the phone from her hand. "I got it Mom. I'll talk to her, but I don't know where he is."

I take a deep breath. I have a feeling this isn't going to be easy so I decide to do what comes naturally—act tough.

"Yeah?" I answer.

I'm trying really hard to sound bored.

"Daniel? I can't seem to find Junior. He's been gone overnight a few times, but never has he taken off for more than about two days. I'm getting really worried." I can hear the desperation in her voice but *about* two days? She doesn't know?

Typical.

I want to ask her if she can remember that time he got beat up by a couple of seniors and he had to go to the emergency room. Had she been worried for him then? Junior told me she didn't even show up at the hospital. He had to ask a stranger for a ride home.

Or maybe she can remember those nights Junior spent here at our house because he didn't want to go home. Maybe she would remember to pay attention to him every now and then instead of treating him like a paycheck.

"Daniel? Do you know where he is?" Her question brings me back.

"No, I haven't seen him." She sighs and waits. Although I know she's obviously worried, I don't feel the least bit sorry for her. She probably wants some money from him or needs him for something. I don't kid myself to think that she really cares that he is missing.

She probably thinks he got into trouble and she'll have to be there to bail him out. She hates spending money on him. Junior only owns two pairs of jeans, maybe three or four t-shirts and a black jacket. And the black jacket we got off a kid last year. The kid didn't need it and Junior was cold.

I'm not gonna offer her anything. So I stay silent and listen to her sigh a few more times. I know she's waiting for me to volunteer to go out looking for him. I refuse to do that. She's his mother. So, I decide to wait it out.

"When was the last time you talked to him?" She finally asks me after a few moments of silent awkwardness.

I take a little time to answer, pretending to think. I know the last time I'd seen him was the day of the accident. I thought I had seen him at the funeral or at school but I know I didn't talk to him.

Heck, come to think of it, I'm not sure if I even saw him then.

"I think I saw him last week at school. I haven't seen him since then."

That's as ambiguous as I can get. I'm really not sure.

"Didn't he go to your house yesterday? The day before that? Your mother said he's been by."

Well, did I want to tell her the truth? I can say *Yeah, he's been coming everyday for the last two weeks and I just choose not to answer the door. Oh yeah, I threw a Coke at him a few days ago.* Maybe that's what she is looking for. Instead of telling her the truth I say, "Yeah, he's been by, but I've been busy. I haven't talked to him."

Again, the sigh. "Do you think you know where he is?" she asks.

"No, I have no idea," I answer.

My mother is still looking at me. I guess she thinks I should offer something else. I shrug at her. "I really don't."

"He's been worrying me lately. He is always talking about the accident—"Great, now she wants to talk about it. I'm not putting up with this.

"Look I haven't seen him," I say, feeling a little more agitated.

"I just wanted to say that he's been talking about death. I don't know what's gotten into him. He said it was his fault and no one's talking to him. He said he was going back. Does that make any sense?" she asks.

I don't care.

"No, it doesn't make any sense."

I guess this is answered too quickly for her and it seems like now she is getting agitated. "Look, I just want you to think about it. You were his best friend. Can you at least ask around? It's the least you can do since you don't talk to anyone. He needs you." The last is said with a gasp.

I have to bite my tongue; I really want to lay into her but I'm doing my best to make sure I keep my mouth shut until she says, "Randy's gone. Maybe you should worry about someone other than yourself!"

"Seriously? YOU are asking me to worry about someone else? Where were you when Junior was sent to the hospital? Or better yet, where were you when Junior needed a mother? You have no idea what you're saying to me. It's called neglect. Look it up. I know what happens in your house! I know what you—"

My mother grabs my arm at that moment. Looks me in the eye and whispers, "You will not make that woman feel any worse than she already does. Who are you to do that?"

She takes the phone out of my hand, looks at me again with so much disappointment that I have to look away, and quietly, without another word, walks away.

I slam my door as if that's gonna make them say *Oh ok, you slamming doors? You have to be right, now*—never works though.

I throw myself on my bed and think about what she said. Where was Junior going? He could be going to his uncle's house. Sometimes he went there when he was upset and I wasn't around, but . . . I'm sure his mother must have called there first. Maybe he was going to the park, our favorite hide-out but . . .

No, that doesn't make any sense.

He must be going back to the plateau. That's the only place I can think of.

Great.

I had no intention of going out there. I'm not gonna go looking for him because I know that's what he's hoping for. He has to learn to stick up for himself. Fend for himself. Something.

I'm tired of always having to be the one to get him out of a jam. In school once at the end of the year, he kept telling these seniors at a basketball game to shut up. The basketball game was freshmen versus seniors.

The freshmen, myself included, were winning, which was really pissing off the seniors. Junior wouldn't keep his mouth shut. He was totally asking for it. He sat in the gym making fun of the seniors. People around him tried to get him to shut up, but he wouldn't. He kept on and on. I even noticed it from where I was.

I saw a guy by the name of Bruce, a.k.a. Mongo, who is tall and muscular, climbing the stairs after him. You would think Junior would be afraid, but he wasn't. If anything, he just egged Mongo on even more. I knew I was going to have to intervene or do something. I wasn't going to let one of my guys get beat up even though I knew Junior deserved it.

It would've looked bad on my image. The game was almost over, yet Junior kept taunting.

Mike tried to get him to shut up because he knew I would get involved if it got ugly, yet Junior didn't seem to care.

After the game as people were filing out of the gym, Junior ran over to me excited about the win. I thought it would end with that, but then Junior calls Mongo a "hairy gorilla" (which was true), only he added some great blasphemous words to the beginning.

It was enough to send Mongo over the edge.

It was a pity too because I really like Mongo, but I had to do what I had to do.

Mongo and I fought that day in the school parking lot. Junior screamed and laughed, but didn't once acknowledge that it was his fault.

Now this?

I don't see why this would be any of my business anymore. Junior and I aren't really friends, he's always just there.

His mother seems to think we are best friends, though, which is kind of strange. I guess I have to think about that. Randy was my friend, my true friend. Junior's just always there.

Junior was always there, looking for a big brother, relying on me, and always following me around like a little puppy.

Damn.

I'm gonna have to go looking for him. I don't want to though. I'll just end up getting mad at him all over again.

Maybe Mike can go with me to stop me from beating the crap out of him. I think Mike will go. We can go pick Junior up and dump him at the house. I figure it will all be over in an hour—two tops.

Or will it be?

17. Déjà Vu

Asking my mom for the car turns out to be a piece of cake—that is after she learns that I'm going out looking for Junior. She shoots me a smile and hands me the keys. I'm not about to acknowledge that smile. She doesn't need to know what I'm going to do to Junior after I find him. The important thing for her is to bring him home.

It's cold. With Thanksgiving around the corner, stores have already started putting up their Christmas decorations. Saturdays are always lazy, but it seems like there are lots of people out at the only store in town. It's really buzzing. People waiting till the last minute to go shopping.

As usual the drag, as we young people like to call Main Street, is full of cars driving around honking at each other. Besides going to school, I haven't really been out in two months. I can't believe time has gone by so quickly; it seems like just two weeks ago we were getting ready to go camping. I guess I have been in my own world these last few weeks.

Mike lives on the outskirts of town right next door to his dad's auto business. They seem to be pretty busy too this time of year. Mike's dad has people lined up outside waiting to talk to him.

If they knew how he treated his sons maybe they wouldn't come here. Then again, he is cheaper because of his sons, so they probably know it and don't care.

I drive into the only remaining parking space. When people notice me, they stare. I guess this is my fault. In a small town, when people don't see you for awhile they start to talk about you. They don't have anything better to do with their time than to talk about people who keep themselves secluded (like me) or bad things that happen (like with Randy). They probably make up all sorts of things about how he died or who he was. I don't want to know. It'll just piss me off.

I get out of the car and keep my head down as I head for the door. Walking into the business, I think, is even worse. All heads turn in my direction when the little bell above the door chimes. I don't bother to look at them, but I can feel the stares as they bore down on my back.

Mike's brother is behind the cash register. He is already trying to contact Mike. I can hear Mike ask again and again who is here.

Joseph is Mike's younger brother. He looks a lot like Mike, but he's much more outgoing. Girls really like him and he seems to have a lot going for him. Too bad about the father though.

Mike walks into the office from somewhere in the back and gives me an awkward smile as he looks over his shoulder several times.

Okay, what's up now?

Wiping his greasy hands on a dirty towel he says, "Hey, Daniel? Whatcha doin?"

I impatiently brush my hair back with my hands. "I need you to come with me to find Junior. He's missing and they can't find him. I think he went to the camp." These people don't need to hear anything more to get the gossip flowing, so I wait to say more until we're out of the office.

Mike continues looking behind me as I tell him what's going on.

"When do you want to go?"

"Now. I want to get this over with. I think he's at the mesa and I think I'll kick him when I see him, so you need to come with me."

"Uhhhmhhh," Mike says with a nod. He's pensive for a few moments. "We can go in a little bit. I'm almost done."

This is exactly what I want to hear.

"I'll help you so we can hurry."

"No, why don't you come back in a few minutes?"

Definitely, something is up. What's going on? I look at him closely and he quickly puts his head down and starts kicking some imaginary rock on the ground. I'm not leaving without finding out what's up.

"No, I'll wait here. I don't have anywhere else to go." I walk past him and enter the work area. They have six cars in the garage, each with parts missing and a few with body parts grayed and wrecked. His father, brother, and two other workers are busy on each car. Business is certainly good. I catch his father's eye and he throws me a crooked smile but never once stops working. He looks like a nice guy and looks like he is a good father, but, well, we all know better.

"What car you working on?" I ask, still walking away from him.

"I'm working on that Chevy over there."

I walk towards the old beat-up yellow Chevy. It looks like it has spent lots of time in garages. It's old, the paint is chipped, and the seats have tears through them. Something about the car is familiar.

"What's wrong with it?"

"The timing chain is off. I already dropped the engine so now I need to align the valves. He tried to start it but the timing chain was broke. Screws up the timing. Lucky, he didn't throw a rod. Makes it harder."

"When did you start on this thing?"

"A couple days ago. We've been real busy."

He still continues to look around as if he's looking for someone.

"So, whose car is this?" I ask, looking around as well.

He does the imaginary rock thing again, but keeps his mouth shut.

Obviously, he doesn't want me to see something. "What do you need me to do to help?" I sit down and stick my head under the trunk. It looks like a mess. I'm not much into fixing cars. Better yet, I don't know that much about cars except maybe what I've learned from Mike and my dad. That isn't saying much.

Once, Karla's car broke down at Pizza Hut and we stopped to help her. Mike wasn't with us—it was just Randy, Junior, and me. We popped the hood and just stared at the engine as if the answer to the problem would show itself or jump out at us. It didn't. It never does, but we looked good. We wiggled the battery cables and checked the oil. Nothing seemed to work. Luckily, her uncle stopped to help and took over. It was good though because for a half an hour or so it looked like we knew what we were doing. Girls seem to like it when a guy knows how to fix things.

Timing chain? I don't even know where that is . . . well, I kinda do, but not what to do with it. I hear Mike talking to someone, and it sounds like he's getting angry. I slide out and can't believe who's standing there.

Kenneth.

Why would he be here? Suddenly it hits me. Mike is nervous and I've seen this shitty car before. It's Kenneth's old car.

I get up, glare at him, and take a step closer. Kenneth doesn't step back as a pansy normally would. He stands his ground. "I want to go with you to find Junior."

I stand stock still. He has taken me completely off guard. After a few seconds, "What do you have to do with him? This is none of your business."

Anger is filling me to the core and all I want is for him to say something that will justify my slamming him against his shitty old car.

"Junior's been coming over to see me. I have to help."

What is the world coming to? Why is Junior going to see him? Junior doesn't even like him. I can't believe this gutless fool. He will say anything to get closer to me.

"Junior would never bother with you. He has better things to do with his time."

"You mean like go knocking on your door everyday? Or maybe he likes to have Coke thrown in his face!"

Kenneth is pushing my buttons. I grab his shirt, push him into the car, and lift him off the ground just enough to show him I can.

"You don't know anything about Junior. Who the hell do you think you are?"

"I know more about Junior now than you ever did. At least I answer him when he needs someone," Kenneth argues. He keeps his hands down but in no way backs away from me.

Mike's father must have heard the commotion because he's now yelling at Mike. "Get them out of my shop. We're too busy for this shit!"

Mike says a few things to his dad, I release Kenneth, and we all walk quietly towards the door. We've made a scene. There are people in the office that have come out to take a look.

"If you know Junior so well, where is he?" I ask when we are near my car.

"I didn't know he was missing. I called yesterday, but no one answered. I don't see him everyday like you do."
Sarcasm.

Kenneth begins to get into my car.

"Wait a minute. Where are you going? You're not getting in my car. No one needs to see me with something like you. Get out!"

Kenneth glances at Mike.

"I said he could go, Daniel. If we find him he can talk

to him. I don't think he's gonna want to talk to you," Mike explains, ignoring my negative nods and getting in the front passenger seat.

Great, déjà vu at its best; this is gonna be like old times. We gotta go out there again with this idiot slowing us down. I sigh as loud and as obnoxiously as I can while reluctantly getting into the car.

We drive in awkward silence for a few miles. I try to get my mind off the fact that this loser is stinking up my back seat. I'll have to get it fumigated. I glance in my rearview mirror and see Kenneth looking pensively out the window. He turns toward me . . . and winks.

I slam on the brakes and roughly guide the car to the shoulder.

"What are you doing, Daniel?" Kenneth asks with a bored look. "We need to be there while the sun is still out."

I grab at the door to yank him out of the car. I want to rip the door off its hinges to get to him faster.

Mike must realize what I'm about to do because he puts his hands on the door and doesn't allow me to open it and kick his butt out.

"Look, Daniel. You need to stop doing this. What's important right now is Junior. Kenneth said Junior wasn't doing too good. We need to find him," Mike says.

"He knows what he's doing. Junior wants attention. He's fine."

"Daniel, not everyone is out to get you."

"I didn't say that. It's just Junior, he'll be fine."

"Daniel don't you hear what we're trying to tell you? Junior isn't alright. We need to find him."

"You didn't even know he was gone. You didn't know until I came to get you."

"You're wrong. That's part of the reason Kenneth was there. He wanted to go too and we were going to leave when you showed up," Mike says, getting back into the passenger side.

I glare at Kenneth through the window and fantasize that I have pulled him out and taken my time beating him to a pulp. He just patiently looks back at me. I grind my teeth and slowly get back into the car.

It takes us thirty minutes to get within walking distance of the plateau. We'll have to walk at least a mile or so. There are no direct roads or even a dirt road that can get us any closer.

I get out quickly and set off in a swift pace. Damn, this feels like déjà vu. My feet are still a little sore and my wounds have just begun to really heal, so I have to take it a little slower than I want to.

"Don't lag too behind fatso, we need to hurry and I'm not waiting on your fat ass," I say over my shoulder.

"I can keep up," Kenneth mumbles.

Mike doesn't bother to reply. He grabs a bottle of water and sets out behind me. Randy isn't here this time. No one is going to wait or baby him this time. Of course, we aren't walking nearly as much as we did last time.

After fifteen minutes of hiking, I can hear the loser's panting behind me. He's really struggling to keep up. I know it's only a matter of time until he stops to catch his breath.

I'm slightly sweating, which surprises me, but I guess that's what happens when you stay in your room for weeks. I am, in no way, like the dummy behind me.

Even though Mike doesn't even break a sweat, he won't pass me.

"How ya doing back there, chump?" I pick up the pace. He doesn't say much, probably doesn't have the breath for it. It's only gonna get worse.

I underestimate the time it's taking to reach the place. We look to be halfway there, which is good, but at this pace we aren't going to be there by sundown. I definitely don't want to get caught out here at night without boots, flashlights, or something to protect myself.

"We need to go faster. It's getting dark," I say, pointing at the sun.

On instinct, they both turn to look, then quickly turn and walk much faster than before. Obviously, I'm not the only one thinking about survival.

No one says a word for the next few minutes. We're too busy focusing on running. I can't see if Junior is up there or not.

"Junior!" yells Kenneth. I don't think he's looking forward to climbing the hill. He's slowing down, gasping for breath, and turning red.

I stop, get his attention, smile and wink. He rolls his eyes and I start to climb. Someone is gonna have to go up to look and see if Junior is up there. Judging by the way no one is stopping, I guess we're all in for a good climb.

After a few minutes of climbing, I catch sight of something gleaming between two rocks. I slowly make my way toward it hoping it's something I can make useful.

I reach for what looks like a silver flask, but stop short. I can't see straight. I just stupidly stand there for a few minutes.

"What is it?" Kenneth asks, coming toward me with Mike right behind him.

I say absolutely nothing; I can't.

"What? What is it?" Kenneth asks again.

Mike looks at it, bends low to pick it up, and quietly walks away. He doesn't answer any of the questions spewing from Kenneth's fat mouth. We begin our climb again, this time at a steady pace.

I have been so angry with Kenneth, so very focused on the idiot that I forgot about Randy.

I forgot. Me.

Suddenly, I dread being here again. I don't want to go up there. I don't want to see the blood splattered on the ground. *Will it still be there? Did they clean up the place before they left?* I never really thought about what they do when an accident happens. Maybe all the bandages and blood-soaked towels are still on the other side. Maybe that's what Junior is up there looking at—if he's even here.

I look around and can still see Randy and me laughing

at Junior as he races to use the restroom. I can hear our fake bragging about all the women we had . . . right.

I'm really gonna beat up Junior now. It's not going to be easy for him and all the rage and anger suddenly makes me move.

I'm on a mission now: find Junior, kick his ass, and throw him from the fast, very fast, moving car. I can see myself keeping Randy's request eventually, but this is too soon. I could have had a whole year to prepare and to forget. Junior has only given me two months.

I pass Mike and Kenneth easily.

I'm the first to reach the top. I'm the first to see Junior standing near the ledge, the first to see the bottle of whiskey in his hand, the first to see the crazed look in his eyes, the first to see the smile that doesn't reach his eyes and the first to see the gun he's holding in his other hand.

18. Junior Has a Gun

"What are you doing, Junior?" I ask after my mind gets a grip on the situation. What the hell is he doing here with a gun?

He doesn't turn around. He doesn't acknowledge me when I call out to him several times. I don't approach him. I'm not about to give him a target.

"Junior, we've been worried sick!" Kenneth yells as soon as he reaches the top and catches sight of him.

I put my hand out to stop Kenneth as he tries to walk around me. I can tell he's ready to say something or do something stupid like hit me, but the look in my eyes stops him short. He doesn't go any further.

Bearded and ashen faced, Junior waves us off with the gun in his hands. I didn't even know he could grow a beard, but irregular patches of what looks like a beard cover his face. He looks like a homeless guy after a rough night.

We watch him for what feels like hours. We're too afraid of what he might do if we move.

No one says a word. I hope he will just turn around,

smile, and say *Okay, we can go now, here's the gun…*

Not gonna happen.

Kenneth is the first to open his stupid mouth. "Junior, how've you been? Maybe we can go get a pizza or something. Maybe, go get a drink—a nice stiff one. Just . . . j-just get away from that ledge."

Great.

Leave it to Kenneth to think about food at a time like this. I roll my eyes at him and give him a shove as I pass by him.

"Junior, look. Your mom is worried sick about you and she wants you home."

"You think I care what that woman feels or cares about?" Junior yells.

This is obviously the wrong thing to say. I can see that now. Okay, he doesn't want to talk about his idiot mother and I can't see him wanting to talk about food, so I try something else. If I can just get near enough, I can grab him and get him away from the ledge.

"Junior, how's school going? We're almost there. Almost at the end of the school year. How about going and getting a drink with us?"

Nothing.

He takes a swig out of the bottle and sways from side to side, contemplating God knows what. I realize he doesn't need to leave this place to get a drink.

"Junior, lets go home. It's getting dark," I plead.

"Junior we need to try to get back down so we can see where we're going on the way back. I don't know if we can find the car at night," Kenneth tries to reason.

"Look, Junior, we need to get back. Let's go so we can get back to the car." I try for the stern approach and take another step toward him.

Mike knows what I'm doing. "You think, maybe we can get out of here Junior? My dad really wants me to finish the cars he has lined up."

Mike tries to position himself on the other side of him.

Maybe between the two of us we can get him out of here alive.

Kenneth's like a statue. Probably scared to death, he doesn't want to get involved. Why had he made such a big deal to come? When it comes right down to it, he's a pansy, just as I've always suspected.

"Junior, lets go home. We'll go to my house and watch some television. We can watch whatever you want. Hell, I'll even let you touch the remote," I say.

"You think I care what you say now? I've been to your house. You don't care about me. Don't stand there and pretend. I've been to your house. What did you do then?"

He takes one step closer to the ledge along with a long swig of whiskey. He turns to me and points the gun, "I'll tell you what you did. You threw a damn soda at me. You didn't care enough to even answer the damn door. Whatcha doing here now? Mommy send you out? Great hard-ass Daniel being told what to do by his mommy . . ."

Junior sure gets courage out of that whiskey bottle. I know if we were anywhere but here, Junior would not be saying what he's saying.

"Of course, Mommy tells you to come out here, and there you are running out here fast as you can to save little old Junior from himself again. What? You think I can't kill myself without you? I can, you'll see. I don't need you."

Closer now, I can smell the alcohol and the stench. He smells like toilet and wet dog. Much, much worse than the usual.

"You don't have anything to say? I see what you're doin and I'm not gonna l . . . l-l . . . let you."

He takes a step back and slips. The bottle falls, making Junior grab for it and fire the gun.

He actually has it loaded.

I grab for his hand and he yanks it away causing another bullet to zip past me. That one had been too close.

"Kenneth!" Junior's hoping for some help.

With his focus temporarily thwarted, I lunge.

Junior again yanks away from both Mike and me. His feet stumble backward.

Junior's eyes grow to giant round orbs, surprised at the fact he's actually falling.

I can't let him fall.

We can't have this happening again. I throw half my body over the ledge and grab for anything I can to grab.

Mike does the same.

We have him. I've got him clutched by the back of his pants (with serious pressure on his crotch) and Mike has him just barely by his shirt.

Precariously, he desperately gropes for us. I guess he's changed his mind about suicide or maybe he just wants to get that serious wedgie I'm giving him out of his ass. It all happens so fast.

"Kenneth, get your fat ass over here and grab him. Help me get him over the edge." I have to make him move. I have to make his coming out here worth it. He hasn't done a damn thing.

"I've got him!" Kenneth says panting. He grabs Junior around the waist. I guess he squeezes a little too hard as we pull him up to safety because Junior lets out a loud belch before throwing up all over Kenneth's shirt.

I sit there on the edge of the cliff taking deep breaths then go in search of the gun.

When I find it, I unload the thing before Junior can get his hands on it again. I couldn't care less if Junior continues to throw up on Kenneth. In fact, I find it to be somewhat satisfying.

"I want my gun back," Junior says, getting up and wiping his mouth.

"You're stupid if you think I'm gonna give it back to you so you can accidentally shoot one of us."

"I just want it back. I'll have to give it back to my uncle."

"Junior there's no way I will give you back this gun. Don't bother."

"What do you care anyway? You don't care about

me. You just want to be left alone. You care about no one but yourself."

Here we go again. I roll my eyes at him. "Junior, I just kept to myself. I didn't do anything to you. What are you complaining about? I didn't do anything to you. Aren't you glad I've left you alone?" I can't believe he's trying to blame all of this on me. Typical Junior, though. I should have known he was going to blame this on anyone but himself. I fully expect him to blame this on Randy.

Randy, you died so now all the stupid things I do or will do are directly linked to your death. People do that all the time. They get molested, grow up in the wrong side of town, have a crack addict for a mother, so . . . the evil things they do in their adult years, even if it's twenty years later, are a direct result. Load of crap.

"You can't blame this drunken stupidity on me Junior. I don't care what you say, this isn't my fault!" I yell at him.

"You were like my brother. You were the only person I could count on. You and I've been together for three years now and you go off and start ignoring me? What do I have left? Nothing, that's what."

Mucus and spit run down Junior's chin as he puts his hands on his face and throws himself on the ground. He mumbles over and over again about friendship and brothers.

I roll my eyes. "Look, Junior, this is all on you. I didn't do anything to you."

"You don't think you did anything? Daniel are you serious? I thought you were supposed to be some kind of intelligent freak of nature or something. How can you be so stupid and smart at the same time?" Kenneth accuses.

"Who you calling stupid, fat ass? You stay out of this or I'll show you the bottom of this cliff." I get up and start to pull Kenneth off the ground by his collar. Mike and Junior also get up to try to stop me.

I shrug them away and start to drag Kenneth toward the cliff.

"What are you doing Daniel?" Mike yells.

"You can't do this!" Junior yells at the same time. Mike grabs Kenneth's legs and pulls them in the opposite direction. Junior keeps yelling the same thing over and over.

I can think of nothing but sending this worthless piece of space over the edge. No one will miss him. I see a split second of fear in his eyes and I feel that familiar satisfaction as it starts to rumble in my gut. I have missed that wonderful feeling. It always did make me feel better.

But then Kenneth does something that I never saw in him.

From somewhere inside of himself, way down deep past all that fat, he finds courage. I see it the moment he finds it. It is a change in the look in his eyes and it takes him a few seconds to find his voice. "What are you gonna do Daniel? Throw me over? You won't do it. You feed on the scared and the weak. You make others around you feel like they ain't worth shit. You get people to rely on you then you treat them like nothing. You don't care about anything but yourself."

I lower him down further off the cliff and shake him. "You don't know anything about me. You're the same person I stuffed in the locker last year. You're talking your crap now only because you think the guys here are gonna save you. They won't and if I threw your sorry ass out—no one would say a word. No one knows you came out here with us. You won't be missed by anyone but your mom."

Kenneth is calm now. A little too calm.

"You can't hurt me Daniel. Not anymore. You can throw me off this cliff, you can kick me around if you want, but you will not hurt me again."

I laugh in his face.

"You read that somewhere didn't you? Maybe it was that very popular handbook, *How To Deal with a Bully 101*. You're pathetic."

"Quit it, Daniel, just quit it." The desperation in Junior's voice brings me up short. I don't need Junior trying to jump again after we've just saved him.

Junior sulks to the ground, puts his hands on his head, and quietly lets his tears fall. I immediately let Kenneth fall to the ground just shy of the cliff's ledge.

"Oh, crap Junior. Are you crying?" I find a large rock as far from him as I can. I don't want to hear him crying like a girl. Kenneth makes things twenty times worse by patting him on the back and talking softly to him.

"Sure, Junior, cuddle up with Kenneth. Perfect," I say to no one in particular.

Kenneth tells him to ignore me and mumbles a few more things that I'm sure are all about my wonderful self. I don't think I can handle the nausea that is starting to form in the pit of my stomach.

I search for Mike. I didn't notice him sneaking off.

It's getting really dark. Luckily, the sky has cleared up just enough for the moon to peek through the clouds and give us some much needed light. The temperature is going down quickly and getting darker. There is no way we will be able to get back now. There are too many predators out looking to fill their bellies, and as slow as Kenneth is—well let's say we won't get far.

The unstable rock and boulders on the way down alone will be more hazardous than the predators. With the luck we've been having out here, one of us would probably get hurt and the others would have to carry the injured person to my car. Of course, it would be Kenneth. He's the heaviest, the dumbest, the slowest, the weakest, and many other est's I can think of.

Although, if he did get hurt, I would love to leave him out here. I'd love to just teach him how this isn't his place. The others wouldn't let me though. I'd end up arguing with them about it, and then they'd want to stay behind. I'd have to leave them behind. It's just not worth the trouble. We'll just have to stay the night here.

I can't see anyone coming out here to save us either. My dad is out of town until tomorrow night. There's no way I am going to ask my mom to walk out here. I don't want to have to bother her or anyone in the family.

We are men. We'll be alright.

Mike has a few brothers, but by the look of the shop earlier, they aren't gonna be allowed to leave. They will be working non-stop way into the night.

Junior's mom? Nope.

I can only handle one dose of that woman a month and I'm well over my limit. She'll come out here with Junior's uncles and start yelling at Junior for putting her through all the trouble of worrying. Besides, Junior looks like he's had more than half of that whiskey bottle and is in no way up to facing her. Kenneth's mom is nothing like my mom. No point getting her to come up here.

No, we can tough it out here for the night. We've done it before, but, well, we aren't prepared for the night. No fire, no blankets, nothing.

Mike must have gone through the same thought process because he's busily collecting twigs and brush. He's finding more than I thought he would. There aren't but two or three mesquite bushes up here.

"You bring a light?" I ask him, picking up brush nearby.

"Nope, but maybe one of the guys did." He shrugs and walks away to find more.

Not me.

I will not be wasting my time collecting twigs only to find out that it's useless.

"You guys have a light?" They're still holding each other and cuddling up as if they are both freezing.

Disgusting.

"Hey, you two Twinkies have a light?" I ask a little louder.

"Don't you have a heart? You'd think that you'd think twice about what comes out of your mouth after what happened today." Kenneth's getting braver, releasing Junior and coming towards me. "He's calling for help, he needs us. All of us. I don't know why, but he needs you too. And you can stand there . . . ."

"Yeah, I'm thinking about today's events—I'm trying to get us some heat. We ain't going anywhere tonight Einstein. We need a fire. And before you get on your high horse again you need to think about what you say to me. I only have a little bit of patience for you."

Startled, Kenneth takes in his surroundings and realizes that it's getting dark. His eyes bulge suddenly as the full impact of our situation hits him.

He puts his arms around himself—well, what he can cover—and shivers. Smart pants hadn't remembered to bring a jacket.

"Yeah, smart cakes, you ain't wearing a jacket. Those flimsy clothes you decided to wear today's gonna hurt you when the temperature falls. So, I'll ask again. Do you have a light?"

"I don't have one. Junior you got something?"

Junior keeps his silence and puts his head down and the tears start to flow freely again. I give him a nudge with my foot.

"Junior you bring a light or just the gun and booze?"

"Don't kick him!" Kenneth cries, suddenly standing in front of Junior.

I laugh at him. "What are you gonna do?"

I take a step closer to him. "That courage you found earlier still thrumming through your veins? Feel lucky?" I have been waiting to use that line. I heard it on television somewhere. It sounded cool.

Now, though, in the situation we're in and with Junior on the ground sobbing like a girl, well, it has suddenly lost its steam.

But I'm not going to tell the pansy that.

"No comment? Junior . . ." He refuses to look at me. "Junior? Junior look at me." Gradually my voice rises until he finally lifts his head with a whisper.

"No."

No one had brought a thing to light a fire with. How

were we to know, that talking Junior down was gonna to take so long? There is no way we could have known. We aren't smokers. I consider myself too smart to pollute my body like that. Beer, however, is a completely different thing.

We came back to this place completely unprepared to deal with our circumstances.

Again.

19. Spoons

Mike comes over to us with his hands full of kindling and throws them on the ground. He doesn't look at us but continues to make a pile. He then gets some rocks and creates a circle. Obviously, we never used all the kindling we had gathered that first day on our camping trip.

"Mike, you might as well quit. We don't have a light to start any kind of fire. These dimwits didn't bring anything."

"You didn't bring anything either, Daniel," Kenneth says, walking over to the grieving Junior again.

"No one's talking to you. Keep your trap shut and go hug that loser."

Mike doesn't interrupt us or stop what he's doing. I guess Mike is more a doer. He isn't ready to give up and it seems like if there is any kind of emergency, he's the guy to step up to the plate. It probably comes with the package of having a dad like he does. Stressed and under pressure is a daily routine for him. It teaches him to focus when others are going crazy.

The way he handled the accident with Randy is something that bothers me. That should have been me taking control like that. I should have made sure Randy had a tourniquet on his leg before I left. Better yet, I should've stayed and made Mike run to get help. Maybe with the things I've learned about first aid, I could have done more. I know how to make a tourniquet, a splint, and even a board.

I've heard of people sky-diving when their parachute doesn't open and they still live. Randy fell probably 40 or 50 feet, nowhere near the sky level. Why would Randy have to die while the sky diver lives? Maybe the sky diver had the right people there at impact. They didn't freeze up and stop thinking. They didn't run away without thinking or run until they couldn't recognize their feet.

Nope, it was just me, so Randy hadn't stood a chance.

"I think I can make a fire Daniel," Mike says, shaking me. He's been calling me for a few minutes, but, of course, I was ignoring everyone. It's what I'm good at.

"How you gonna do that?" I figure I'll at least help with the circle he is trying to create and begin rearranging the rocks.

"I saw a movie where this guy used a dried tree branch and a board. He rubbed them together and smoke came up. It didn't look like he struggled too much."

"Yeah and it was a movie. He probably had someone there with a cigarette lighter. I read that a man tried for four days to make a fire that way and it worked only after he figured a pulley system. I don't know if I can recreate what he did, but I'll need a rope to try." Looking for a rope, I leave them behind. I can tear up my shirt or pants, but it's already getting pretty cold out here. I don't want to risk it not working because then I'd be out of some warmth.

I look for what seems like an hour to no avail. I can't see very well anyway. There could have been rope all over the place, but I can't see it. I can't find anything. When I reach them again, they're still in the same position. Can you believe they're still hugging and Junior's still crying? I'm focused on the job at hand and I'd rather not be without warmth out here for the entire night. It's only gonna get colder out here.

"I found something like a rope under that boulder over there. I've been trying this since you left but I can't get the smoke to even appear and I'm getting a blister." Mike's wiping his brow with his hands and trying his best to stay positive.

"Let me try to wrap this rope or whatever this is around the twig." I make a figure eight on the thin dry branch holding it on one end and making Mike hold the other. My idea is to use the rope to make the branch rotate faster than it would if I'm just using my hands. I, too, have seen many movies where they rotate the twigs to create fire. I think it's the friction.

We work at this for what feels like hours. Both Mike and I are sweating now and still there's nothing.

Kenneth, who has been quietly watching us says, "I think there has to be some air under that board so that the fire can catch."

"What do you know?" I say but look at the board again. We haven't made much of a dent, so something isn't right. I review the board again and inconspicuously use my shoe to move the board just enough to allow air beneath it. Kenneth coughs a little, but I choose to ignore him. I will not give him the satisfaction.

"I remember, in that movie you talked about, Tom Hanks had some shavings. Maybe that's what we're missing." I use my trusty Swiss Army knife to whittle one of the twigs down.

After a few minutes I have about a handful. I don't think we need that much, but I'm not gonna take a chance of not having enough.

"All right, Mike, let's see if it works this time." I place the shavings under the twig and start trying again.

Nothing.

For what seems like another hour we try. We don't even get any smoke. Sweating and getting tired, I figure we had better spend the rest of the night trying to find somewhere to get a little sleep. Kenneth is getting colder. If I admit to anything, the cold is probably why Kenneth is hugging Junior. He's cold.

"We can't get this fire going. We'll be all right out here if we get some sleep by that boulder over there. There's some wind coming in through the north, so if we stay on the south of it, we should be fairly protected." I'm not waiting for them to follow me. I march purposefully to the boulder and plop myself down on the ground, edging as close to the rock as possible. It's getting colder by the minute and although I have a heavy jacket on, the wind is still slicing through it. While I was working on trying to start the fire, I didn't feel the cold, but now with the wet perspiration settling on my shirt I can definitely feel its sting.

Mike and Kenneth help Junior walk over to the boulder. He isn't crippled, but he sure is milking it.

Mike lies down for a few minutes, but suddenly bolts straight up.

"What is it?" I ask, thinking maybe something has bit him.

"Pliers!" Mike answers with a smile.

I'm not sure where he's going with this. Pliers? Maybe he has some magic pliers or something. I don't understand what he is so excited about.

"Give me the gun," Mike says, sticking his hand out.

"I'm not giving you the gun."

"Look, I'll show you what I'm doing. Hopefully, it'll work."

"Why do you want the gun?" I answer, refusing to give up the gun.

"I walked out of the garage and I didn't put my stuff on my table like I usually do, so I have pliers, and I think I can make a fire."

Reluctantly, I hand him the gun. I have no idea what he's up to, but I trust him.

Mike ejects the magazine clip, catches it in his hand, and unloads the gun with his thumb like he's some kind of expert. Makes me wonder what else goes on at his house with his father for Mike to know his way around a handgun like that. He looks up at me and smiles, but it isn't a humorous smile. It's one of those smiles that tell me he knows what I'm thinking.

Mike quietly but efficiently takes his pliers and squeezes the tip of the bullet casing, causing it to come off. Inside is gun powder. Of course.

Understanding dawns as Mike repeats this same deconstruction to ten more bullets. He walks to the kindling we've created and pours it carefully into a pile on top of a flat piece of dry bark.

"Stand back. Hopefully this will work," Mike says with a smile. He's really enjoying himself.

"Wait, isn't this dangerous?" Kenneth asks, standing up and getting close enough to look down at the gun powder.

"Don't you listen dumb ass? You're gonna lose some of that fat if you don't stand back. It'll just melt right off." I laugh.

Mike doesn't wait for him to answer, just unlatches the safety and raises his arm. Kenneth and Junior quickly run away behind me, of course.

The gun discharges with an earsplitting smack and makes everyone, including me, jump.

Nothing happens. No smoke, no fire, nothing.

"The shot must have gone wild," I say.

"No, something's missing," Mike answers.

We talk for awhile about what could be done to make it work. At this point, we only have two more bullets left. We can't risk losing another one until we talk through it.

Kenneth and Junior sit quietly near the boulder, not really looking at us.

"Why don't you try putting something on top so that it'll make a spark?" Kenneth suggests suddenly joining us.

I don't bother to say anything to him because he does have a point. I fleetingly think of throwing his ass in there and creating my own spark, but his fat would just absorb the impact and then we'd be left with just one bullet.

"Daniel, why don't you put a rock on top? That should make a spark," Mike suggests.

I place the rock just as he asks and pray that it'll work. I'm really getting cold now. In the back of my mind, I hope it doesn't snow. That would be our luck.

"You want me to do it?" I ask him.

"Nope, I can get it," Mike answers. Confidence is just bubbling out of him now.

He raises the gun and shoots at the rock. Immediately, fire sparks on the gun powder and soon the kindling begins to smolder. I run to it and begin to blow slowly in an effort to keep it from dying.

It doesn't. The flames rise as we put more wood on to make a huge bonfire and enjoy the heat.

After a few minutes of warming ourselves, we settle down for the night hoping the fire will last, but Mike suggests we sleep close together so we can stay warm. Kenneth hears none of this because he suggests, "I think we should all sleep close together. We're gonna get cold and if we sleep close, we may get a little more warmth." Kenneth moves close to me.

"You would like that wouldn't you?" I move away from him and get closer to Mike.

"It's not about you Daniel. Junior doesn't even have a jacket. We all need some warmth and no matter how tough you are, you're gonna need warmth too." Kenneth moves Junior closer to Mike and lies down next to him.

"Junior's so drunk right now he won't even feel any of the cold."

"So what? It doesn't mean that he doesn't feel anything." Kenneth puts an arm around Junior to prove his point. "You can stay over there but I'm gonna try to keep him warm."

"With your fat ass you could keep us all warm." I laugh at my joke but, unfortunately, no one else does. Not even Mike. He just turns his back to everyone and tries to get some sleep. "You gonna spoon Junior all night long?"

Kenneth sighs and doesn't bother to answer anything. He turns his back on Junior so that Junior's in the middle. I'm left alone to fend for myself. I take off my jacket and use the sleeve as a pillow. Normally, we would have stayed up until the wee hours of the night talking, but no one seems to want to talk. Considering our situation, I don't really want to prolong the night. I just want the night to be over so I can go back home and to my room.

"Don't you ever get tired of trying to be tough?" Of course, it's Kenneth who breaks the comfortable silence. "Don't you sometimes feel bad for what you do? People have feelings and some of the things you do now could affect people's lives for years."

I'm tired of his whining voice. I lean on my elbow. "Look, Kenneth, just because you think you can say things now, doesn't mean I can't hurt you later."

"What are you gonna do? Hit me? Push me in a locker at school, send a shitty text to everyone about me, trash my house? I told you already, you can't hurt me anymore. I'm past that."

"Oh, I can hurt you all right. I think what you're trying to say is that I can't touch you mentally but you're wrong. I will always be able to hurt you. This conversation alone is proof. You can't let things go. You're always looking to me for approval. You're always defensive about the things I say. You pay attention, all right, to what I have to say. Don't lay there and think you're something because you finally found some courage in that shabby body to say something."

For a few wonderful moments, I feel like I finally made him shut up.

Nope.

He whispers, "I've always said things to you but I'm not going to fight you. You think the answer is in violence and it's not."

Junior moves to face me. "Can't you just stop for a little while?"

I smile at him. It's about time he woke up from his pity party. "It's about time you get your head out your butt Junior. I was beginning to think it was gonna stay there forever."

Kenneth sighs so loud Mike turns to look at him. "I

think you should stop while you're ahead. You're only gonna make it worse."

"See, now Mike. He has lots of brains." I rearrange my jacket and try to get some sleep.

"How come you never answered my phone calls or talked to me?" It's barely a whisper. At first, I ignore him. It takes me awhile to register what Junior has asked. Kenneth mistakes my silence for refusal to acknowledge the question.

"You're not gonna answer him?"

"Stay out of it or I'll make you sleep over there," I say. I point to a lonely small rock that will offer little to no protection.

"I just don't understand why you didn't answer me when I tried talking to you. I can't believe he's gone. I can see his face and the blood—the smell of it. Every time I close my eyes I see it. How do you do it to be so—like you don't care?" Junior's sobbing again. The tears stream down his face like rain. I can see them even in the faint light from the moon and fire.

I'm not sure what to say or even if I want to answer him. What *can* I say that won't make him feel worse? Do I even care if he feels bad? Will it make things worse?

Looking at his face now, I'm smart enough to know that if I say the wrong thing it will definitely make things worse.

Next time, maybe we won't be on time. Next time, I could be going to Junior's funeral.

The look he shoots at me stops what I'm gonna say. He looks miserable, confused, and desperate for something. And that something is *something* I can't bring myself to give him—not now and maybe not ever. He's obviously hurting and looking for comfort.

Why do I have to comfort him? I shake my head in the dark. That is a job for someone like Kenneth or his mother. Kenneth looks to be doing a first-rate job of it. Junior's mother, on the other hand, doesn't care about anyone but herself. She will offer nothing but incriminations.

I'm not a psychologist—like Mrs. Hinho—but I think that something like that will have long lasting affects. That will definitely qualify for the bleeding hearts.

Bleeding.

I can still picture Randy falling. I hear the crunch of bone, hear the thud of his head hitting the rock. I can still see his shattered body lying lifeless on the ground. I can even remember me standing there—useless.

I had done nothing.

"You're not gonna answer me?" Junior accuses, bringing me back.

"I wanted to be left alone and you didn't get the picture. Why do I have to answer the door? Why would I need to answer your calls? I was alone in my room doing nothing. Why are you mad at me? Don't take your drunken behavior out on me. You have only yourself to blame." I don't feel the need to talk anymore. I want to sleep and get back to my room. I'm always very content when I'm there. I have no one to answer to.

"You answer the door because you're my friend. You answer the phone to see how I'm doing. That's what friends do." He's getting braver with every word. With his voice rising he continues. "You should be there for a brother; you should have been there for me. I wanted to talk—"

"I didn't." It's that simple.

I'm not going to answer any more questions. No one's gonna make me do any of those things and no one (especially the weak pansy and the crybaby) is gonna make me do anything.

Junior asks lots of questions over and over again and I pretend to be asleep. He asks about Randy's sister and Yna. He wants to know how she's doing. He wants to talk about the good things Randy had going.

He talks about Randy and his football highlights. How once he had gone home after making a game winning touchdown and there were three cars waiting for him. A different girl in each car.

How Randy had once stepped in for Junior when another guy had pushed him. How Randy was so in love with Yna but didn't want anyone to know it.

He talks about the relationship Randy had with me. How we were so close that we knew what the other was thinking, especially on the football field. We never fought. We knew each other since grade school. Our mothers were good friends in high school. We followed each other around and were never apart. He even talked about the first time he started to hang out with us.

I can't even remember that. I forgot that Junior was once one of my victims. He had been in the restroom one day in 7th grade when I happened to be giving Reggie a wedgie. The fact that it rhymed had everything to do with Reggie's pain. Junior had come in, seen what was happening, and quietly tried to walk right back out. Randy caught him at the door. Our attention moved away from puny little Reggie and on to Junior. I had put his head into the toilet a few times and I was gonna beat him up a little when Randy suddenly had a touch of sympathy for him. He told us to stop and after a few punches, we did. For some reason Randy had liked him.

Don't know why, but Junior became a pest around us, never leaving our side. Then he just started to hang out with me more than with anyone else. I think it's because he was so much crueler than any of us and liked the fact that no one would hurt him anymore. He became sort of protected.

But is he still protected?

Yes, he is.

Everyone thought Junior and I were best friends. They saw us together all the time. He practically lived at my house. No one is gonna bother him. He will have my protection through high school no matter what I do. Now, anything beyond that is an entirely different matter. I don't see us attending the same college. Heck, I don't even see him getting accepted anywhere.

Maybe this sudden pity is because he's alone now. I move around enough to peek at him. He has stopped talking for a few minutes and is still smashed between Mike and Kenneth.

No, he looks to be passed out. I think the whiskey finally did him in. All is quiet. I have to admit that I'm feeling pretty cold now. The comfort of body heat is given mostly to Junior. I contemplate getting closer to Mike, but then I'll in turn get closer to Kenneth—nope. Not gonna do that no matter how cold I get.

Sleep eludes me. I shift my position several times but can't get comfortable nor can I get any warmer. My body starts to tense up and I have to focus on breathing to make it relax. I read that somewhere. It's all mind over matter. So, I perform my counting strategies and start with relaxing my fingers then my toes. Relax the head and shoulders—

"What was that?" Mike yells. He's up on his feet quicker than lightning.

Startled, I move quickly to see if I can catch a glimpse of something crawling or an animal of some kind in the moonlight. Kenneth shifts a little but also springs to his feet. Images of scorpions coming for revenge travel quickly through my head as I wonder what has freaked them out. I can't see a thing.

Kenneth turns around as if trying to see his back.

"Is it still on you?" I ask coming towards him.

"I'm wet," Kenneth murmurs quietly.

It takes me a few seconds to figure out what he's talking about. I'm still unconsciously looking for a creature to come after me when slowly, as if in a wave, the realization dawns on me and I can't help but laugh—hard. I howl with laughter while Mike and Kenneth argue about the warm wet clothes between them. They look at Junior and he seems to be sleeping like a baby.

"Well, don't look at me! I'm not spooning with you guys now," I snort.

It's priceless. Something they will not live down for a long time. The good thing, if there is a good thing, is that it's only piss. Think about it.

If you piss yourself, the gang will talk about you for weeks, maybe even months tops, but if you crap yourself, we'll talk about you for the rest of your life.

But then they both do something unexpected. They start

laughing too. It's all too surreal and crazy. We're stuck out here with little warmth trying to save a crazy kid who's trying to kill himself. After all we've been through, each of us in different ways, it's too much to take in.

After we have our good laugh, we fall asleep, and even though we try to take as much heat from the fire as we can, it's still very cold and I thank our intermittent luck that we even have a fire. Sleeping in tight little balls trying to get as warm as possible, we finally fall into a restless slumber.

20. The End to the End

We climb down the plateau as soon as daylight peeks through the clouds.

Mike and I practically carry Junior to the car (no easy feat, believe me). He looks to have one heck of a hangover. He can't remember much of anything. He continues asking for his gun. I'm not quite ready to give that up. Junior throws up twice in the car inside of a Whataburger cup we find in the back seat. What looks like popcorn fills up the cup, so I end up having to pull over to pour it out. No way am I letting that stuff spray the car.

We don't speak much on the drive home. Each is lost in thought. I've decided to take Junior home first, hoping to lessen his dim-witted mother's worry.

The road to his house is full of old cars parked on the sides. Junior's house is covered with old wooden siding, the paint is cracking everywhere you look, and there are cars parked around the house that look to have been there for more than fifty years. Some of the windows are covered with duct tape.

Walking up to the house, I realize that the crumpled forms on the patio (or what looks to be a patio) are really passed out people. Beer bottles are thrown about and someone is snoring rather loudly just inside the house.

His mother comes to the door with little on and opens a screenless screen door. She smells like rotten eggs, her white tank top and black bra are covered with grease stains, and her teal shorts are barely visible under the rolls of fat. She's disgusting.

Because we're still carrying Junior around, she thinks at first that he's hurt.What looks like concern passes fleetingly across her face, until she realizes he's okay. She then grabs him roughly by the hair and asks him where he's been.

He closes his eyes and whimpers like a hurt puppy. She yanks harder when he says nothing and pushes him to the ground. Up to this point we've done nothing, but when she starts kicking him in the head I have to step in.

She yells, "Look at you, all high and mighty with your friends. You're gonna be nothing, just like your dad." And she kicks him again.

I position my body between them and glare at her while Junior struggles to get to his feet. He wipes his bloody mouth on his sleeve.

"Don't get blood on your clothes you ungrateful shit. I buy you enough as it is," she yells as she tries to get around me to kick him.

I very calmly grab her arms, "You will not hit him again, Mrs. Saenz." I gently push her back. I have refrained from using our nickname, Mrs. Insane. I can't see that the comment will help at the moment.

Scrunching her face with anger and rage she turns to me. "Who the hell do you think you are getting in front of me and my son?" Spit comes out of her meaty mouth as she says the words and then tries pushing me out of the way. Some of the drunks have started to stir. Mike, sensing what might happen, stands closer to me. Kenneth, surprisingly, has done the same.

I should know better, the little voice in my head I frequently ignore whispers not to—but I do it anyway. It's rare that I listen much to it anyway.

I kick her square in the ass when she leans over to pick up the broom. She falls forward but catches herself on a board jutting out of the house. She glances back at me. She can see the anger and resentment in my eyes. I hate this worthless wench. She should never have been allowed to reproduce.

She says nothing. I expect her to yell or call for help and get some dumb drunk that can stand to beat us all but she doesn't. We stand closer to each other, and Mike places Junior behind us. I think she knows she's beat for now.

"Get out!" she mutters.

She turns and walks away. I notice one single tear escape from her old face. She's young but the years have not been kind, so she seems much older. It's her hard life. She has no one to blame but herself.

Before she can leave, I know I must get her to understand. Purposefully, I walk behind her, grab her arm and whisper in her ear, "If you ever touch him again in anger, I promise to come after you. You have to sleep sometime."

If she's astonished or incredulous, she doesn't show any signs. I turn and tell the guys to get back in the car.

Leaving is obviously a relief for Junior, but I'm not sure what's going to happen next. Where will he go? Keeping him at my house would require a serious talk with Dad. Mike's house is out of the question for obvious reasons. His dad won't hesitate to use him as a punching bag just like the rest of his sons.

But Kenneth solves the problem. "Daniel, can you please drop me and Junior at home?" His use of the word home is meant to imply that it will now be Junior's house. I look at him in the rearview mirror to see if I have mistaken what he said. Just yesterday he winked at me and I wanted to beat the living snot out of him, but today he gives me an understanding nod. That's all I need.

Junior will be okay, his mother will bake those great cookies for him, and he'll survive. I make myself a mental note to visit Junior tomorrow.

After all the drama we've seen these last two days, talking seems useless.

I drop them off quickly, eager to get home. I need to be at home by myself. I want to be alone. Too much has happened.

Mike's father is outside already working on a car when we drive up. I hope this won't be another repeat of Junior's mother. I don't think I can stand anymore BS. "Look, maybe we can check on them tomorrow after school, just to make sure Junior's okay," Mike says, reluctantly getting out of the car.

"Yeah, I thought the same thing. I'll see you at school and we'll go together."

"Alright."

Mike slams the door and walks into the house without speaking to his dad. I guess he's trying to avoid the questions or a fight, but with his dad it's inevitable. Why do people have to be so shitty to their kids? They shouldn't have any if they're going to be that way.

I round the corner and see my mom.

She's waiting for me on the front steps. My need to be alone is squelched when I notice her wringing her hands. "Your father came home early last night, *Mijo*."

Well, hell. Let's add more to my plate.

She's obviously worried because I didn't make it home last night. "Where were you last night? Why didn't you at least call?"

Nope she's furious. I can tell exactly when the worry has turned into anger. "We were up all night thinking the worst, your dad even called the cops. Do you know how embarrassing it is for your father not even to know where his son is?"

I slowly walk up the front porch and open the door to find my father sitting on the couch looking at me. He has his work clothes on already and it seems like he's just waiting for me so he can go back to work. He turns his cowboy hat in his hands several times but says nothing for several minutes. Usually, I would kind of tell on myself, spit everything out like throw-up and tell him more than I needed to, but after the day I've had already and the last few months, I feel like I don't owe him (or anyone else) an explanation.

Who is he to question me when I know I'm doing the right thing? Junior would have killed himself had I not gone looking for him. Mom even told me to go help. I'm simply following orders.

"Where have you been? No, don't start telling me about how it's justified. There's nothing you can say that will make this okay. There are phones now. All you have to do is pick one up and you can let us know where you are."

My dad rises from the sofa to stand before me. He's calm which is a bad thing. It means that he has already made up his mind for punishment and all reasoning with him is out of the question. This isn't good.

Knowing this makes me keep my trap shut. Talking will only make things worse and I'm sure not gonna tell him about Junior's mom and me kicking her in the ass. That won't help my case just now.

"You're getting older and I don't want your mother and your *little* brother here alone. If I hadn't come home they would have been. It's time to grow up and get that head of yours out of what happened with Randy. Enough is enough."

He calmly walks away, but it's getting hard for him to keep his cool since I refrained from saying anything. Suddenly, he turns to me, "You won't go anywhere but school for a month. I don't want to hear that you did this again. I'll be gone for a few weeks. Be the man, son."

I know he's angry. He isn't one to lecture, but instead just says little things that make me think about all the crap I've done. He's not like this with everyone.

He once found out that the man he'd been buying tamales from for the past year was leaving out one tamale for every dozen bundle. He was selling eleven tamales and charging for a dozen.

Dad thought it was an innocent mistake until he opened up the other two small bundles. He was so angry he took the tamales back and threatened the man. But he didn't raise his voice once. Simple intimidation was all that was needed. We haven't paid for tamales in at least a year and a half.

He has a way with things. Whether by force or by intimidation, he will get his point across.

I figure a month at home is a great thing because I can stay locked in my room and there's no need to have to talk to anyone. It will be great.

"You will clean the garage and mow the lawn and anything else your mother wants you to do. No questions asked." He turns and walks quietly out the door.

I get to my room and throw myself on the bed. So much for enjoying my time off; he's just given my mom the green light to treat me like a slave. I know she'll do it too because in my mom's eyes there are always things to do.

I don't bother getting up again until it's time to go to school.

21. Changes

School the next day is the same but different. The classes are all the same, the teachers are the same, the smell is the same, the teacher's voice has the same whine, but some things are different. I can't figure out what, but something has changed.

Maybe it's me.

I don't beat anyone up in the restroom but I don't avoid the place either, which makes a few of the kids nervous. There are lots of students avoiding me in the hallways too and if I enter the restroom, it's amazing to see everyone leave so quickly.

Junior and Kenneth are nowhere to be found at school. I look for them in between periods but finally give up when I see Mrs. Hinho trudging toward me.

Mike and I have one class together and all we say to each other is that we'll meet after school. Other than the brief exchange of words with Mike, I manage to make it through the day without talking to anyone. I think for sure Ms. Hinho will call me in for another enlightening session, but she hasn't.

Oh yeah, Ms. Hinho's name is not a testament to her character (or maybe it is.) That's something I don't ever want to know. She's never been married and she's never had any children. She is however, in my humble opinion, a hen. Other than a fat pudgy cat, she reminds me of a hen, a mother hen—especially the cackle/cluck part.

Luckily, I have survived another day without crossing her path. I know I won't be so lucky later, though. The odds of her forgetting about me are slim to none.

I meet Mike after school and we drive in my car to Kenneth's house. I remind myself that we aren't there to be friends with Kenneth and that we're only there for Junior, but I don't really believe that.

My feelings for him have changed somewhere along the way, but I'm not sure when. Maybe it was when we found Junior or maybe he's simply like a fungus that is growing on me. I prefer to think of the latter option because I can handle that better.

When we pull up, both of them are in the yard pulling weeds and putting down mulch.

The grueling work and the sweat pouring down their faces isn't something I'd skip school for, but Junior's smiling and working like he's on fire.

"Hey, guys. What are y'all up to?" Kenneth asks with a smile on his face.

A smile?

What is happening to this world? He's greeting me with a smile and I'm coming over to his house.

I ignore him and look at Junior. "We just came over to check on you. Wanted to see how you were doin'."

"He's doing fine now," Kenneth answers for him.

"I was asking Junior. Not you," I say. I'm still not looking at him. I kind of feel bad. I'm not sure why.

"I'm okay. I didn't go to school today. My mom came by. She wasn't too happy about me living over here. It seems that if I don't live at home she doesn't get child support." Junior looks up at me and grins. "Go figure. I didn't even know she kept in touch with my dad." Junior piles some mulch on the garden bed.

I can't believe it. I've never even heard of Junior's dad paying so much as a cent. Of course, this is his mother talking. She's a cruel woman and selfish.

"You talk to your dad?" I'm shocked but hopeful.

"No, of course not. She's just embarrassed more than anything else. People are gonna find out I'm not living with her."

"You gonna try to get in touch with him?" I watch Kenneth and wonder what he's looking at as he looks toward my car. I glance over to it to see if there's something wrong, but as usual the car is green and ugly. He is weird, what am I thinking?

"No, I won't bother. What for? He never bothered," he shrugs. "How much effort you think it takes to get money taken out of your check?"

I shrug back at him.

"He only did enough to make himself feel better."

"Yeah, well . . . we just came over to see how you were doing." I glance over at Mike to see his take on things. Mike's shrug is enough to tell me he's shocked too.

"You wanna come in? My mom's cooking dinner; there's plenty." Kenneth's question is aimed at me. He doesn't glance at Mike or Junior. He's testing the waters to see if there is any change in our relationship.

I look at him for what seems like a long time. I can't figure out whether or not I want to be his friend. Do I want to cross that line with him and call him a friend?

After all that's happened in the last few weeks, it seems like somehow he has become a part of my life without my really realizing what has happened. He was there when Randy was killed. He was responsible for Randy's climb. Randy invited him on our trip.

Is it my jealousy? Is this something that stems from

Randy or do I really *not* like him?

No, if I'm brutally honest with myself, I don't think Kenneth intentionally wanted Randy to fall from that cliff. It isn't jealousy. That vicious truth is harder to cope with. If he wasn't responsible for Randy's fall, then who is? Me?

Still.

I'm not ready to be buddy of the year to him, but I somehow don't want to hurt his feelings mostly because he's taken in Junior.

Junior is suddenly important to me. I think the whole world is different. Everyone is changing. I care about what happens to Junior, what happens to Mike, and maybe even others. Maybe I always did care.

"I can't stay today. My dad's grounded me for not coming home." I lower my eyes not wanting to look at him anymore. I want to leave.

"Maybe tomorrow or something," he says with a smile.

I can't believe what I do next. It's completely unexpected and it takes both Junior and Mike by surprise.

I smile back at him.

I think about turning away but decide to go with it. I will be okay with all this eventually and the awkwardness of all this will get better. I hope anyway.

Mike squeezes my shoulder and we walk quietly to the car.

Strange how things change.

* * *

Again, my mother is waiting for me outside when I get home, again wringing her hands.

Damn, what now?

I hesitate going into the driveway. Maybe I can just turn the car around and leave, but I know it'll make things even worse. Whatever those *things* are.

"Hey, Mom. What's up?" I ask.

I jump out and slam the car door. I'll have to get that fixed. It takes three tries this time to close it.

She's silent for a long time just watching me. Okay, this is pity.

"You alright, *Mijo*?" she asks.

She touches my head with the back of her hand. She's never that worried about my well being. I mean, she cares and all, but I don't ever see her asking about my health. It's just one of those things that's taken for granted.

"Your dad, *Mijo*..."

She says nothing after that and a cold shiver goes up my spine. Something's gone horribly wrong.

I don't move a muscle hoping things will change or that I will never have to hear what she is about to say.

"He was in a car accident. He's in the hospital."

It's worse than I think. My breath leaves my body and my eyes can no longer focus on what's in front of me. After all the shit that's happened—what now?

"He's going to be okay they said, but he looks bad. He said he wants to see you."

She's still wringing her hands. Is there something she isn't telling me?

"Are you sure he's going to be all right?" Anger is filling my blood. She isn't telling me the entire truth. It's too obvious she's keeping something from me.

She shakes her head slowly, "You need to go. Now."

22. Hospitals Suck

The ride to the hospital takes only five minutes in this stupid small town but it feels like forever. I break ten traffic laws and then run a red light. I figure the cops can just follow me to the hospital if they see me, but luck is on my side—or is it?

On the way, I don't think about my father. My mind shuts that off completely. My mind, instead, drifts to my friends and to those people that hurt them. Am I any better than Junior's mom? Mike's dad? I hurt those around me all the time, yet I can look at that worthless woman and that fat jerk and think only of how horrible they are. What does that say about me? Am I that bad? Is this why Randy died and why my Dad is now in the hospital with God-knows-what wrong with him? Something has to change.

I drive up to the hospital, park quickly, and run across the parking lot.

Then I change my mind. My pace slows.

I don't want to know what has happened. I just want to be oblivious. The urge to turn tail and bail is almost overwhelming. I have to force myself to go through the double glass doors.

Hospitals are like schools in that they all smell the same: disinfectant and death mingled with urine. I hate the smell.

We once spent weeks in the hospital when my grandmother got sick. We would sit in the waiting room and play cards for hours.

She slowly died of diabetes as her body gave out one organ at a time. We played the roller coaster waiting game. It was one of the longest three weeks I'd ever had. I hate the hospital. Then again, I don't know many people that love it. It's the same with schools.

A pretty girl from school flips through magazines at the circulation desk. She wears the candy-striped outfit with the old fashioned nurse's hat. Her eyes dart to and from the floor looking a little embarrassed when I walk up to her. Normally I would have flirted a little, hell, maybe a lot, but flirting is the furthest thing from my mind.

"I'm looking for my dad."

There's no need to say anything else. Everyone knows everyone here, but my memory fails. I can't remember her name and her hair is covering up her nametag.

"He's in room 206. Elevator, second floor, down the hall, and to the left." I have to strain to hear the end of it. She won't even make eye contact. Is this because of my dad's condition or is she just shy?

I want to ask her how my dad is but I'm afraid.

Me.

The tough school bully is afraid. Things change all the time. What's next? My house burning down, my brother or Junior dying or Mike? Maybe Kenneth? What else is going to happen? I'm exhausted. I'm done. I don't want another day to start because that'll mean something else is gonna happen—so far everything bad. Now, here I am walking as slowly as I can to the elevator.

No.

I'll take the stairs. It'll give me a chance to think about things.

Wait, I don't want to think. I want to know what's going on. The stairs will be quicker anyway.

I take the steps two at a time and try my best to hurry. My dad wants to see me.

I make it to the nurse's station and quickly ask for room 206. All nurses seem to be alike. This one is no different. She's chubby and smells of smoke. Something about nurses and smoking.

"Room 206," she says not bothering to let me finish my question. She pisses me off with her shitty attitude but now is not the time.

The door creaks as I slowly push it open and although I've run every horrible scene through my mind on the drive over. I'm totally, overwhelmingly, numb-shockingly unprepared for the sight of my father banged up.

The huge bed swallows him up and makes him seem helpless and weak. My father is none of those things, but he sure looks vulnerable now. His entire left leg is raised in a cast and the tubes and machines attached to him are too many to count. The lump in my throat grows. I will not lose it here.

"Hey, Dad!" I try my best to act cheerful, but it seems hollow even to me. My voice seems out of place.

He opens one eye but because of the swelling is unable to open the other. His failed attempt at a smile makes my heart ache.

"*Mijo…*" he mumbles.

I grab his hand and squeeze. Why do we have to die? This life would be better without all this pain. Things just feel out of whack—like they'll never be the same again.

Life here will never be the same. It's already changed so much and I guess things aren't done changing.

"They think I might lose my leg."

My breath leaves me again and suffocation begins to set in. Change sucks.

I can't imagine my father as an invalid. He's struggling with that realization as his one uninjured eye ventures in the direction of his leg. That's why mom looked so worried. What will he do now without his leg? How will he survive not being physically strong?

No.

There's no way God will allow this strong courageous man to lose a leg. *He* cannot be so cruel as to take a best friend and my dad's leg all at the same time. It's so unfair.

"You're going to be alright, Dad. You'll see." That lame comment is all I can think of to say.

"You'll have to be the man of the house now for sure. You need to listen to your mother while I'm here and no more taking off without telling anyone where you're going." He takes a deep unsteady breath. "And son, I love you. I want you to know that and I'm proud of you. You've had loss and you've tried to deal with it. I know it's not easy."

Words escape me. I don't know what to say. He has never told me he loves me.

Never.

Never once in my life has he ever shown me that he gives a crap. I'm at a loss, he never even made it to one of my games, but here, now, in this room, I'm paying attention to every word he's saying. For once, I want to make him proud of me.

This sucks.

Our conversation is almost nonexistent after that but I remain in the hospital with him in comfortable silence for what seems like hours.

I find out bits and pieces from his conversations with the doctors. He was on his way to work when an eighteen-wheeler ran a red light. My dad swerved just enough to miss getting t-boned. The truck swiped the tail end of his work truck. He swerved, smashed into an electric pole, and smashed his leg. He's obviously lucky to be alive.

This is all so random. Randy's accident was random and my father's accident—also random. Junior's really wasn't but had he fired the gun just a little to the left, it would have struck me in the face. Everything in my life is random. How can a person be sure of anything? I used to think my life was so ordered, structured even, but it's not. I thought I was in charge. Why did Randy have to die? My thoughts swim erratically in my head.

Nurses, fat chubby ones, continually come in to check vital signs and to move him around. Relief fills me when they make me leave before they change his catheter. Seeing him more vulnerable than he already seems is something I don't want to handle right now.

Finally, he turns to me and tells me to go and check on Mom. Exhausted after the emotional roller coaster, I slowly make my way to the exit, yet I'm not eager to go home and answer Mom's questions.

The doctor comes in before I leave to let us know there is no change so far in the condition with his leg, so I really don't have much to tell Mom anyway. Friends and family begin arriving, so I feel it's okay to leave. I need time to be alone.

Walking out through the automatic double doors, I glance in the direction of the front desk and wonder if that girl from school is still there. (Jessi is her name or maybe Jessica.) The desk's empty.

I wonder what I would've done if she were still there. Would I have talked to her? I think so. She's cute, and, well, nothing can be done about Dad until we find out what's going on anyway.

I'd like to think I'd be Mister Suave and talk to her a little, flirt, and then ask her out on a date. I haven't thought of girls in weeks. Funny how things change.

Lost in thought, I don't recognize the car parked next to mine until Yna emerges and quickly blocks my car door. She isn't leaving me a chance to ignore her. I wouldn't have ignored her anyway. I guess I need to face things head on and stop hiding.

"Hey, Yna," I say, leaning against the car. I figure she'll

start to ask me questions about the accident or something, so I brace myself.

"How's your dad?" she asks, toeing the pavement. I'm not sure if she's being shy or if she doesn't know how to ask whatever it is she feels she needs to ask.

"He's gonna live," I answer. I'm not giving her more than that. We both know she isn't here for that anyway. I'm sure she cares but that isn't the reason she's standing before me.

"Good, I heard about it from my mom." She's silent for a long time. I figure I'll give her time to work up the courage.

"You think of him?" she wonders, still toeing whatever it is she's fixated on.

I have to think of a way to answer her without sounding condescending. Of course I do, every second of the day, even in my dreams.

"Sometimes," I look at her in the face and try to figure out what exactly she's really trying to ask me.

"I'm sorry I was so mean to you. You know, at the funeral," she says. She puts her head down and tears start to well up in her eyes.

Great.

I guess my sigh's a little louder than it should've been because her head jerks up and she glares at me like she wants to whack me in two. In no way do I want more tears, so I explain, "Look, if you're worried about that, don't be. I've got thick skin."

She shoots me a weak smile. "I've been thinking about that for awhile now. I can only imagine what you're going through. For awhile, I thought only of myself, and then I saw you going to your car by yourself. You looked so lonely."

I hate that she watches me. I hate that others undoubtedly feel pity for me. I'm a loner now. If she sees me in that light then others do too.

"I know you guys were close. I see you now alone," she says.

I'm starting to get angry. Is that what she wants? Does

she want to make me feel worse than I already do?

"Look that's not what I wanted to tell you. I just wanted you to know that I'm sorry for yelling at you and I wanted you to know that—that I know what you're going through. Maybe not in the same way, but I feel it too," she explains. She puts her hand on my arm and squeezes. She's trying to reach out. It seems like others are trying to do the same.

I don't really think I deserve any of it. I know what I am, what I've been for years.

Now what am I? All I feel is regret.

"It's okay, things are gonna get better. They have to." I shrug and give her the same weak smile she gave me. Things have to get better. At this point they can't get worse.

"He loved you like a brother. He did. He talked about you all the time. He used to talk about you guys going to college together," she laughs. "Heck living next door to each other."

Her eyes well up with tears again.

"Look, you were the one, too. You were the one he planned a future with. All those other girls—" It's not my place to tell her about the others, there were many, but he loved her. He always had.

"Those other girls didn't matter to him. I think you know that." I hope to make her feel better. I need her to stop crying.

"I saw those stupid girls at the funeral, covering up his locker. They're stupid."

She smiles at me, "I better go. I hope you're dad is okay."

"I'll see you around, Yna. If you need something or someone messes with you, you let me know." I feel the need to take care of her, for Randy.

"Thanks." She quietly climbs into her car and drives away.

Changes. Nothing is certain but change.

23. Closing the Door

Going to the hospital everyday sucks.

It's a constant strain on my already frazzled emotions. Dad's been in for a week now. I struggle to get a straight answer from the doctors and *We'll have to wait and see* gushes out of the doctor's mouth before they even step into the room.

I find myself getting shitty with the fat nurses and the even dumber doctors. Today it gets so bad that my dad kicks me out of the room after I cuss out a nurse for messing up on his meds.

The stupid woman came in earlier with a pill that looked odd to me. When I asked about it, her face turned red and I didn't let her pathetic apologies spew out of her mouth. Never did find out what pill she had in her hands.

It's too frustrating so I left.

I ride around town for a little while and try to get a grip on my emotions. At first, I'm not sure what I'm thinking, what I'm doing, or where I'm going.

Before I realize it, I find myself at the cemetery.

The cemetery's located a little outside the city limits. Pine trees line the borders. A large iron fence marks the entrance and the words "Rest with the Angels" are marked above the intricate framework. I didn't drive the day of Randy's funeral, so it takes me a few minutes to find his site.

It's there, the only one that still looks fresh. I get out of my beat-up car and don't even care when the door won't shut. I walk slowly to the grave site and kneel before the lump of ground. I wonder when the dirt will be even with all the rest of its surroundings.

It's so eerily quiet out here. Flowers, some fresh and some dead, lie all over the surrounding area. The entire town can be seen from this view point. It's a fitting place for him to be. He'll forever be above all the people here in this pathetic town.

My hands shakily feel the fresh dirt and I dig my hands in. The dirt's surprisingly cold. Randy sleeps down there somewhere—cold.

No, Randy is not asleep. He will never be awake again. He'll never walk with me to school, he'll never throw the winning touchdown and I'll never be there to give him a hand after a tackle. Hell, I couldn't even give him a hand when he needed me most.

Junior was almost in the same place. I would be visiting two burial sites instead of just this one. Heck, my father could have been here too.

That realization is too much for me to take.

I never cried for Randy. Not at the funeral and not even in my room. A lump in my throat the size of a softball increases and I can't figure out what to do.

I suddenly feel like this is just too much and I release all the emotions I've been keeping in. Gasps and gulps come out of me, the likes of which I have never before experienced.

The fear, anger, resentment, and, most of all, guilt try desperately to escape from my chest. I don't hold any of this in anymore. I want what's eating me up on the inside to be outside.

I don't want to do this anymore. I don't want to hurt or to pretend. I don't want to feel any more anger, mistrust or fear. I just want to be me again without all these horrible emotions of loss.

I let it all go. I let go of all of my inhibitions. I cry—no sob—until my chest hurts. I cry until I'm numb all over. I lay there sprawled out on the ground for a long time letting the sun set and wishing Randy would come back and hoping that things will work out for Junior, for my dad.

I quietly begin to talk to Randy and tell him what those stupid girls did to his locker. I tell him what Junior had almost done to himself. I let him know that I wasn't beating anyone up anymore nor do I feel like doing it anymore. I tell him I miss him.

I laugh about our idiotic counselor and her ridiculous cat pictures, my mom's pathetic pity for me. My brother and how he hasn't bothered me for weeks. I tell him about Yna and how much she misses him. I promise to look out for her and to go visit his parents. I promise to come by frequently to visit him and to keep an eye out for Mike, Junior and even Kenneth. I let him know that he was right and Kenneth isn't so bad. I go on and on for a long time and let the calm, spent feelings overwhelm me for the first time since that fateful day when everything I ever knew changed.

I feel at peace and after awhile I haul myself up and slowly begin to walk back. Lost in thought, I don't see Kenneth standing near my car. He grunts once to get my attention, causing my steps to falter.

He's parked his truck outside the cemetery. I wonder how long he's been standing there. He isn't looking at me but at the town. His stocky build looks slimmer than I remember. He leans on my car and waits. I guess he's trying to give me my time alone with Randy. It's a sign of respect that says more about him than anything I can think of.

I wonder how long and how many times he's been out

here. I lean on the car next to him and for several moments we say nothing. Like with my dad, this is a comfortable silence.

"I heard about your Dad. How ya doing?" he asks.

"He's gonna be okay." I believe it too.

"This the first time you been out here?"

"Yeah, couldn't bring myself to do it. You?" I figure he came out here pretty regularly, so it surprises me when he answers my question.

"No, I couldn't do it either. For a long time I thought it was my fault. I was the one that said I would climb that stupid mesa. If I hadn't gone with you guys, Randy would still be alive."

I never thought about Kenneth having any kind of remorse or blame. I'm surprised. I have to admit that I did blame him for a lot of that weekend *and* for Randy's death. I know, better though.

Who knows what would've happened? Maybe something else would have happened. We'll never know but blaming ourselves is something I don't want to do anymore and I don't want to place the blame on anyone else. I'm through with that.

"It wasn't your fault and it wasn't mine," I explain, looking at him. "I was angry at first because I wanted someone to blame and you were an easy target because you were new to the group. Plus, I didn't know you."

"It wouldn't have happened if I had stayed home like you wanted me to."

His face contorts with pain and I can see the remorse in his eyes too. He reminds me of Yna.

Someone like Randy dies tragically and it doesn't just affect one person. It affects everyone around. It sucks. I'm so selfish.

"I'm through with the blaming game. We need to close those doors," I sigh. "Don't get me wrong, I'm not ever going to forget him, but I'm not locking myself up in my room anymore."

"I was wondering when you were going to stop doing

that. I think Junior's a little worried about you."

I sigh louder, "Junior needs to worry about himself. How's he doing?"

"He's fine, all things considered. I haven't let him drink anything. He probably drank enough the other night to last him a few years. His mother sucks. She calls all the time but my Mom has loads of patience with her. Junior says she'll go away eventually. Especially when she realizes that we aren't gonna take the child support away."

"He should take the money just to teach her," I say.

"I told him the money was his, but he doesn't want anything to do with either one of his parents," Kenneth says.

I nod my head, thinking of that raunchy, smelly, revolting old woman. I would hate to have her as a mother.

We stand there in silence again. I can't get over the changes in everything. Kenneth and I actually have a conversation that doesn't involve my wanting to stuff him in a locker. Hurting people around me isn't something I want to do anymore.

My father and I look to have a different relationship and Junior has, hopefully, found a new home.

"Well, how about dinner tomorrow?" Kenneth asks pulling me back to reality. My eyes are still swollen from crying, the snot's still trickling, and I can still feel my chest throbbing but I feel better than I have in a long time.

"Sure, I'll bring Mike over after school. Maybe even get in a movie. That is if my dad's okay with it." I turn around to get in my car and hesitate. Hugging him is out of the question (I've changed but not that much) and I don't want to say something gay, but I want him to know I appreciate him being pretty cool.

I look at him and he nods, sensing what I want to say.

I throw him a nod and get in my car.

"Oh, by the way, my uncle has that car wrecker place outside of town. There's a hinge I found that would fix that door."

I remember him looking at my car earlier and I realize he

was trying to figure out what kind of hinge the car had. "Okay, we can put it on tomorrow."

I take another glance at Kenneth and catch a glimpse of Randy. He had that same easy smile, dark shaggy hair, olive skin. Sure Kenneth is stockier, but there is something there.

Heading home, I can't help thinking about the days ahead of me. It's going to take some getting used to but I think I can handle whatever's coming. I have my friends, my family, and I'm still here. Eyes open.

Finally.

That has to count for something.

* * *

The counselor calls me into her office two days later. The last two days have been great. My father is coming home, his legs are going to be okay and my mom is cooking a big welcome home dinner. All my friends will be there.

My car door had been fixed with the help of both Mike's expertise and Kenneth's parts. Dinner at Kenneth's house looks like it might become a routine on Wednesday nights. His mother is a pretty good cook, Junior has a room to himself for once in his life, and he is able to see what a real home is like.

Sitting in the hallway waiting for her to call me into her office is agony. School offices are always full of crazy activity. The phone rings constantly, the bad kids walk in and out, the principals try to look busy, and parents call or come in to complain about their dumb ass kids.

Mrs. Hinho pokes her chubby face out the door and calls me in. As usual, she's wearing those dangly earrings that she forces to jingle with a bob of her plump head and her office still smells of Ben Gay.

As she sits at her desk, she folds her hands under her chin. "I know you are still going through emotional hardships Daniel. I know you are still having nightmares, worrying about your grades and social situations."

Is she kidding?

I decide again not to say a word. She isn't interested in me, she's only interested in being right. I look around the now familiar office and realize that she probably has a lonely life full of disappointments and hardships. I know I've changed, I know I'm a little more compassionate about some things, my outlook on life is better, but in no way, form, or fashion have I become an ass kisser.

I'm only going to sit here and look at her. Nothing I say is going to change her mind about things. "Randy was such a special person, he was someone that will be greatly missed. I've had numerous young girls and boys come in and shed tears and fears regarding the accident," she continues.

Yeah, I see the lines forming outside of her office. I don't believe her for a minute.

She looks up at me, "I'm glad you're opening up to me more. I knew if I gave you some time you'd come around to seeing things the right way."

She hefts herself up, walks over to one of her photographs that actually has a picture of humans smiling at a beach somewhere and sighs again, explaining, "I tell all my friends all the time the wonderful things that counselors accomplish, especially ones like me who devote our entire lives to the pursuit of our students' happiness."

Is she kidding? I have to force myself not to roll my eyes. I just want to get out of here. Rolling my eyes will only make this last longer and might make things worse. "They don't believe me when I tell them the stories I've heard . . ."

This will end soon, I know it. She goes on and on and on but I stop listening. I look towards the front office and the desolation and quiet atmosphere is concerning. She doesn't look like she has anything to do nor is there a student waiting outside to talk to her. That isn't surprising.

"Daniel? Did you hear what I was saying?" she asks.

She leans over her desk. I don't even attempt to look down.

I wait instead and look into her eyes (much safer). I know she'll ask me the question again.

"Are you feeling better now?" she asks smiling.

I nod as quickly as I can. Smiling as if knowing she's done a wonderful, awesome job at *counseling* me, "I don't think you need someone to come out to your house. I think I've done enough."

Shaking her head and humming, she writes me a note to get back into class. I'm not about to tell her that school is out now and that I'm on my way home.

I leave again without saying a word.

24. What is Normal?

Everyday I feel I can't get out of school fast enough. School is stifling.

Christmas vacation's coming soon and I'm so looking forward to it. I can't wait to see all my family from out of town again and I can't wait to have a little bit of freedom.

Christmas is a huge event at our house. We have people from as far away as Mobile, Alabama coming in to town. My aunts and uncles will be here and they always bring food. Not just any food but the good junk food. It's great.

Thanksgiving passes in a blur because I have my head up my butt. The accident happened the beginning of October. I can't believe it has been that long ago. Now though, I'm anxious to spend the holidays in my room.

I still haven't asked Karla out. I work up to it everyday in Mr. Farts English class but getting her alone and away from her friends is harder than giving up sodas for Lent. It seems like she and her friends have some kind of secret code and when there's a perfectly handsome eligible bachelor in their midst, they flock together like geese or something. There's no way I'll go up to her in front of her friends and I think they know it. What if she decides to turn me down? I'll get laughed at by all those stupid girls.

Anxiety fills me because the Christmas dance is this weekend. Things, however, seem to be looking better everywhere I turn.

The kid in front of me, Andy Wasterwill, never gets picked on anymore, not by me anyway. I pretty much keep my mouth shut. There are times, though, when things will slip out of habit. Sometimes it's hard to stop the vomit that comes out of my mouth. I used to just let it flow, but recently I've become more aware of what I say.

It's not always enough though because one day the dumb kid in front of me asked some stupid question. I was ready to get out of class because the bell had already rung, so I said, "Shut the hell up."

Just like that.

It came out.

I think he was a little surprised because he turned to look at me with both fear and surprise in his eyes. I looked away from him and the other students. I couldn't believe that I had said that. I couldn't tell which was worse. The fact that I had said it or the fact that I actually felt bad about it.

Me.

I felt bad.

I hadn't beaten him up or anything. Well, at least not since Randy had died. My face turned bright red and I was powerless to stop it. It wasn't the fact that I had said what I did and it wasn't the fact that I had beaten him up in the past. It was because I felt bad. What is that? Have I changed that much?

It wasn't but three months ago when I had caught some of these kids in the bathroom and made them all pay for our camping trip. Most had paid several times. What I did had been a lucrative business and I had excelled at it most brilliantly, but now, sitting here in Mr. Farts' class, I am embarrassed for what

I have done. Whatever I was thinking and whatever I said must have worked because this kid hasn't asked a single question since.

A few days later, I ask to go to the restroom in math class. We're going over geometry again for all those stupid people who think they can get the concepts like osmosis so they refuse to study. I don't want to hear them asking the same damn questions over and over again, so I walk out. I try real hard to go in between classes and to stay away from the restrooms Randy and I used to hit daily, but sometimes, like today, I can't stand being in class with stupid people.

As soon as I walk in the door, I'm slammed against it. Me.

I'm slammed so hard against the door that I can't see anything for a few seconds. Dazed with my hands on my head, I struggle to look up at my attacker. A punch in the side of my stomach has me lurching to the ground. Never have I been punched like this. Stunned, it takes me precious seconds to react. Who would dare do this to me? Was I still in the same school? Did I wake up in the Twilight Zone?

I distinguish, from the voices, that there are a few of them. They yell and egg each other on as they take swings at me from all sides. Judging from the voices and the punches, there are at least three of them. Figures, one person could never have brought me down so quickly.

Getting to my feet as fast as I can, I come up swinging. No way am I going down without a fight.

"Daniel?"

In my frenzy to strike back, I fail to register my name. At the moment, striking back takes over my dulled and stressed-out senses. I punch two of the guys square in the face and the third I smack in the neck. That hit takes him out completely.

I learned to fight out of necessity when I was younger. My cousin Ralph used to come over and use me as a punching bag whenever he got the chance and rag on me all the time for being a chubby kid. He taught me to be tough, mean, and to take a punch. He's two years older than me, but big for his age, so the fights we'd have were far from fair and Ralph didn't fight fair. A wooden board to the ribs when you're six years old, for example, takes at least three weeks to heal to a tolerable ache. Needless to say, those beatings only lasted as long as it took me to get older, bigger, and meaner. My revenge was swift and vicious.

"Daniel, is that you?" Greg asks. He ducks away from me.

Pausing and focusing takes effort, and I can't seem to get my mind out my butt fast enough to focus on the idiot speaking.

After a few moments and the realization that there are no more punches headed my way, I focus on Greg.

Greg Valdez is a short, stocky wannabe gangster. You know the type, they talk like they're in the hood (even though we live in this small hick town), they dress with pants that are twenty sizes too big (when they run they have to spread their legs), they use hand gestures to talk (because they're too dumb to learn real words), and they think it's cool to be stupid in school. Well, to be fair, most of these idiots have an IQ just above 70.

Greg has never been one of my targets. I left him alone, not because I'm scared of him (I tower over him by about a foot) but because he never has any money. His parents barely squeak by every month and he wears the same thing all the time. He's not a good target for someone like me. Besides—he wasn't fun to pick on.

Other than little name calling every now and then, I pretty much left him alone.

He has short, shaved hair with a little curly queue embedded in the shave which I know is against school codes, huge black pants, and the Virgin Mary t-shirt.

Typical.

My heart really starts pumping and my nerves are shot and my damn stomach hurts. Someone is gonna pay.

"What the hell do you think you're doing?" I ask him as

I assess the other idiots with him. Two other guys are standing now a safe distance from me, nursing their wounds, and moving slightly toward the exit. They are just like him, nobodies and wannabes.

"What the hell do you think you're doing, Greg?" I ask again.

My focus hones in on him and him alone. I don't care about the other two idiots, they'll feel my wrath soon enough. The taste of blood on my lip feeds my rage. Somewhere in all this, one of these losers had gotten a good punch at my face. My fists tighten and I start to lose focus again.

"We were just askin' for money from some kids. We thought you were one of 'em," he explains as he tries to shake my hand. As if I would do his stupid handshake anyway.

I glare at his hands as if they are repulsive tentacles.

"You hit me." I state the obvious just in case he missed it.

"Sorry, man I didn't know it was you."

The other two idiots quietly leave, but I don't bother to glance in their direction. When Mark enters the restroom, I do.

I realize two things as soon as I see Mark. One: they've told him some lie to get him to come in here. Two: their intent to beat up on Mark is obvious judging from my bleeding lip. Three: (yes a third) I have been replaced.

While I had been trying to get my life back on track and gone into total seclusion, this idiot had thought to fill my shoes. Greg has seized the opportunity to get in on something he hadn't had the guts to get in on before. Now that I was no longer beating up on kids in the locker room, he had quietly and efficiently it seemed, stepped right on in.

I laugh. I can't believe this idiot would think it was okay or, even more importantly, that he could step in to MY shoes. It's absurd to even think of. He's a loser, a nobody, a wannabe. This is trying to take over my territory?

Well, to be fair, I'm not doing this anymore and I have no intentions of going back to it. Hell, I felt bad when I told that idiot in class to shut the hell up. To be fair, someone can easily take up the slack and give these losers what they deserve. If I'm not doing it anymore, then who am I to get upset at someone who's just doing what I had done for so long?

Maybe it's fate that has stepped in to show me that it's okay and things are working out for the best. Keep them honest. Show them how stupid and absurd they are for listening to Greg of all people when he promises them something they both know he isn't going to do.

Mark is a perfect example. Here he is (again) after all that I thought I had taught him. He's so very gullible. He's wearing tight black pants, black t-shirt, and now has what looks to be a new spiky hairstyle. Mark's sporting a new goth look.

Walking away and letting Greg handle Mark is exactly what I'm gonna do, and as I yank at the door, the look Mark gives me stops me short.

It's a pitiful look.

One that says many things all at once: save me or help me being a few of them, but the other seems to be accusing me.

That's the look that stops me. The "help me" look doesn't bother me because he should know better. He should know not to believe people when they promise you something, especially if the promise comes from someone like Greg. Heck, if it comes from someone like me. He's stupid enough to come here, so he gets what he gets for being a dumb-ass.

The other look he gives, now that one does stop me. I can't figure out why he's accusing me of a situation HE put himself into, but now that I'm here, well I guess he thinks I'll save him. Maybe he thinks I'm a horrible person for leaving him here and letting this wannabe get a good hold on him. But the more I look into his eyes, the more I know that's not the case at all.

I know rumors have spread about me not beating kids up anymore. I know people are talking about my seclusion and my new relationship with Kenneth. I'm not taking money from students and I'm not going into the locker room and stuffing anyone in anymore. I've stopped taking lunch money during lunch and I've stopped saying things to students in class. I've even stopped calling people names.

The bully stage of my life is over.

Mark knows this better than anyone and now here he is looking at me like I'm the one that is supposed to help and save him.

No.

I know what it is.

It's the fact that I'm walking away. The fact that I'm not participating doesn't have an impact on him. It's because I'm leaving him here with Greg and not stopping things.

I nod at Mark and walk out slowly.

I'm not anyone's savior. I can't save anyone. Hell I couldn't save Randy. Why would I save Mark? I certainly have no aspirations of being the hero of the school.

Why would I do that much of an about-face?

I read an article once about this kid who was a reformed bully and toured the country explaining to people that he no longer performed the acts of a bully and that he had changed. He talked about his home life and gave reasons for his behavior. He would even cry every now and then to make his messages have a bigger impact. He neglected to mention, though, that he was now thirty-five years old and no longer in school to have the *opportunity* to bully kids. He never went to college either, so there went that.

This guy was making big money and he wasn't even what one would call a "typical" high school bully, but the principle of it is still the same. He wasn't touring for free. No way.

He was still taking money from people, only now he was doing it in a different way.

I'm not going to be that guy.

Becoming a spokesman for dummies that don't learn is not for me.

I almost make it back to my class when my steps

involuntarily slow. I debate on whether or not I need to check on Mark. Maybe he doesn't have any money and I need to let him know that if he continues to promise money and not stand up to someone like Greg, and then he's doomed to face this over and over again. Even if it's not Greg, there will always be someone there to bully him until he learns to stand up for himself, or, better yet, to keep telling someone until the problem is fixed.

I turn around and walk a little quicker back to the restroom. I need to teach him a lesson, but I'm not going to save him.

The closer I get, the louder Mark's yells and pleadings. Some kids never learn. Pleading and yelling for help doesn't do anything but entertain the bully. Greg will feed off that fear. He'll know he can get whatever he wants from Mark and he'll know that Mark will do whatever he asks from now on.

It will not stop.

I slowly open the door, still debating what the hell I'm doing here helping Mark who should know better. The door shuts in my face before I can walk through it. Something (or someone) has been thrown against it. With a sigh, I open the door again.

Greg is punching Mark in the stomach as Mark flails about like a rag doll, not even trying to defend himself.

Damn.

"Let him go, Greg," I whisper through clenched teeth. I'm actually starting to feel sorry for the dummy.

Of course he doesn't hear me and neither does Mark.

Greg grabs Mark by the collar and in one swoop opens the door to a stall before throwing Mark into it. I know what's coming next.

That's it. I can't let it go on. This newly acquired conscience sucks. I charge into Greg's stomach yelling, "Let him go, Greg!"

It's amazing how no one ever hears what goes on in the restrooms. This one in particular is a little out of the way near the gyms. Yes, the same restroom Randy and I called our own. I just now realize that I had automatically come here without thinking about the fact that Randy and I didn't have a specified time to meet. I had just come. Randy would never meet me again.

I hit Greg squarely in the chest, sending him into Mark. Surprise is apparent on both faces and I use it to my advantage. Greg and I are similarly built, but I catch him by surprise so I have the upper hand. I punch him hard in the face and grab his collar just like he had done to Mark.

"You will not do this to Mark. You will not do this in my restroom!" With every word I slam him against the stall.

After the initial shock, Greg gets his senses back, "You don't rule here anymore Daniel."

He was calm, too calm.

"I will not tell you again. I will be back just to make sure you're not here."

I punch him in the stomach for effect. Along with my cousin's monthly beatings, I also had my dad teaching me to fight. He used to say that it's important for a man to show strength.

Greg gasps for air and nods his head. I throw him on the floor and yell at him to get out.

I turn to Mark and I guess he thinks he's next because he lifts his arms in defense. I hear the creak of the door as Greg quietly lets himself out.

I roll my eyes at him. "Mark, don't you ever learn?"

I start to walk toward the door when Mark gets my attention.

"Hey," he whispers.

I stop but refuse to look at him. I can't keep the anger off my face. I want to lecture him or yell at him for being so gullible but I feel like if I start in on him I will never stop. He should know by now.

"I just wanted to say thanks," Mark mumbles when he realizes I'm not going to turn and look at him.

"Why did you come?" I ask him. I have to know what it is that would convince someone to come to the restroom to meet someone like Greg.

"He said you needed me."

Shocked, I turn to look at him. He smirks and gives me a bloody smile.

Perfect.

As if I couldn't feel any worse. "Why did you listen to that? Don't do that again."

I can't help but smile. Why? Who knows, after all that has happened this year, what else?

He smiles back, pats me on the back as if we're old friends, and walks out the door.

I walk out behind him and run smack right into Karla.

Alone.

Epilogue

After

I asked Karla to Prom that year and she went with me. She wore a slinky little midnight blue number that I enjoyed more than you know. We went out for a few years until we had to go off to college. We parted ways, but still kept in touch. She will always be my first love. You never forget your first love.

I didn't beat up anyone, nor did I terrorize any more students in the restroom. Occasionally, I would call students names or make fun of them—nothing worse than what anyone else does. Some habits die hard, but, all in all, it was harmless and people knew it. By the end of the school year, they stopped taking longer routes to avoid me and they had stopped ignoring me.

Mike and I became pretty good friends and hung out a lot with Junior and Kenneth until Mike's dad had a heart attack. Mike was suddenly responsible for his brothers and, because his father was too weak, the beatings stopped altogether. He died shortly after leaving Mike with the business and the house. Mike does well for himself.

Kenneth and Junior went off to college together, something that totally surprised me. Junior ended up living with Kenneth for the rest of high school. It was a good match. I was a frequent visitor at their house even when they weren't there. His mother always had cookies and that special drink ready when she heard I was coming to town.

Junior's mom occasionally tried contacting him, mostly to ask for money or a place to stay. The bank had foreclosed on her house so she bounced around a lot. Who would have thought that broken-down hovel would matter to anyone, but apparently the house was on some property where they wanted to build a shopping center. The shopping center idea never took off, so the place is completely empty and waiting. With the house torn down and the cars towed out, it's an improvement.

Junior's father, to my knowledge, has never once tried contacting him. Probably for the best.

I went back to playing football in high school, but my heart was never really in it. I just went through the motions, more for Randy's parents because they still came to the games. I was glad when senior year came around and it was over.

Yes, I graduated early and went on to college and majored in Engineering. It was, second to that year, the most memorable time of my life. I received a four year academic scholarship.

I come back to this small town every chance I get. During those early years, I never thought that I'd do that, but it's the truth. I have turned into the type of person I used to make fun of.

This place has that special charm every little town calls its own. Everybody knows everybody and rumors spread like wildfire.

It is home no matter how many different places I live. The smell of the rain mingled with limestone, little Mexico, the outskirts with all the new hotels, the prisons recently built that help supply jobs—all these things add up to what I call my real home.

And Randy.

Randy is here. I visit him every time I come home. He has a wonderful lot that overlooks the town. It is a fitting place. I've heard his sister, Lizzie, had a son shortly after graduation and they named him Randy. I haven't seen him, but I hear he's a star at every sport he's tried. It's a good thing.

I get the 411 from my mother and grandmother as soon as I drive up the pathway. They tell me everything I need to know about who's with whom and where everyone is. Most of the time, it's just stuff I don't really want or need to know, but I cherish their talking just the same.

My father has added another two rooms to the house making it now have something like 13 rooms. Crazy, but again its home.

The other day, I turned on the evening news and saw a crying mother at a school in Alabama. She was upset because her son had committed suicide. He was being bullied at school. It was a tragic story and one that, since I stopped what I used to do, was close to my heart.

I realize that we had saved Junior's life and I had also saved Mark, but I couldn't save Randy. Even though Mike had told me that I was his only hope—I know now that I couldn't have really saved him no matter how fast I ran that day.

And even though I didn't do any more bullying after Randy died, I still wonder what would have happened if we had continued on the path we were on. It's a scary thought and one I force myself to face.

I try to put the shame of what I used to do to good use. No, I don't go around and give lectures or talk at schools, but I do volunteer a lot for different organizations. I try to be a positive influence on those around me.

Am I perfect?

Not by a long shot, but I try to live my life right.

For Randy.

For more information and resources on bullying, please visit:

Grelibooks.com

Study Questions

1. How does Daniel know Karla will come back in Chapter 1?
2. How did they get Steve (Steve-O) to show up in the restroom? Did they mean to harm him regardless of how much money he gave them?
3. Who assigned responsibilities for the camping trip? What were they?
4. Why did Daniel get angry when Kenneth didn't want to get in the water?
5. Foreshadow: Before the accident, what happens and what does Daniel think to indicate something bad will happen?
6. Quote a hyphenated modifier found in chapter 13.
7. Quote two similes found in chapter 14.
8. Characterization: Compare/contrast Randy and Daniel. What are the differences in their family lives and their relationships with their families?
9. Inference: In chapter 15, what does Mike pick up from the ground as they make their way back to camp? Why does this astonish Daniel?
10. What is a star athlete? Do you think Randy fits the profile of a star?

Discussion Questions

1. What is a bully? Why do you think they do what they do?
2. Why does Junior put up with Daniel? Why does he continue to come around regardless of the treatment he gets?
3. Kenneth is portrayed as weak by Daniel. Do you think this is accurate? Why or why not?

4. The story is written through Daniel's point of view. Do you think his opinions of people are accurate? How does that change the reader's thoughts?

5. Daniel seems to change his attitude and become someone else without the help of a teacher, counselor, or parent. Do you think it's possible for a person to solve their own problems by themselves?

6. Daniel views authority in what way? Do you think most young adults share the same views toward authority? Why or why not?

7. What would you do if you had an encounter with Daniel and his friends? What would you do to prevent this from happening to someone else?

8. Do you see Daniel's characteristics in another student in your school or someone in your past? What do they have in common? What would you tell this person if you could be sure no repercussions would come your way?

9. Junior's mother neglects Junior in many ways. Mike's father beats him. Do you know anyone with parents like that? How do these students cope? How did Junior and Mike cope with their home situations?

10. Mike turned out to be a level-headed character when he was faced with an emergency situation. How did Daniel, Kenneth and Junior respond? How do you think you would respond? Does anyone *really* know?

11. The characters had a difficult time dealing with the death of Randy. How did each character deal with his death? Have you ever lost someone close to you? How did you deal with the death?

For more worksheets and discussion questions or any other questions, please visit www.grelibooks.com

Acknowledgements

There have been so many wonderful people who contributed to the writing, producing, and marketing of the book. We want to say thank you.

Thanks to my editor, Stacy Kinney, who is absolutely wonderful. She's been supportive, encouraging and a very useful resource. Thanks for your continued support.

Raul Villesca, my website creator and book cover designer who has shown a talent and proficiency that has astonished everyone on this project.

Thanks to our family, for helping us in any way possible and for never saying no. We are forever grateful.

Most importantly we thank God for giving us the patience, perseverance, support, and opportunity to allow our dream to come true.

Turn the Page for a Special Preview
of
The Second Book in
The ME Series

By

MGVillesca

Grelibooks.com

Prologue

I'm sweating. My hands, my feet—even parts of me that haven't seen sweat for years are sweating. I have been trying to get to my destination for the better part of two days. Even my cotton shirt is sticking to me. Can this be possible? Can a person sweat to death?

I shift my carry-on to the other shoulder. It's getting heavier by the minute.

Sitting in the airport terminal and waiting in the packed lobby area is not making things better. People stretch out on the floor with blankets, trying to get a few hours of sleep.

Creeping up on three in the morning, the terminal is full. The snow advisories and the future weather forecasts don't look promising. I kind of hope I'll be unable to make this meeting. Secretly hope that I'll be stuck here for another two days.

It's ridiculous to be so nervous. I run a successful marketing company now. I'm a woman of the world, a woman who has taken her life and steered it in the direction I want. I'm not that dumb little girl they thought they knew so well. I can only think of one reason I have been summoned here after all these years…..summoned.

Yes, summoned, is a good word for what he said. I wish I hadn't answered my cell phone two weeks ago. That call had made my world crash from the perfect life I force myself to lead and turned me into this person who has sheen on her upper lip.

Forced to wait in the airport terminal yet again because of delays, I can't help but wonder what this meeting means. I haven't seen or heard from Jack in over ten years, not since high school graduation. Sure, I've heard bits of information here and there from people I've inadvertently bumped into over the years, but never a face-to-face meeting.

I'm not completely surprised. We all knew it would come to this.

I watch as a young child with pigtails passes by me with her arm comfortably attached to her mother. She's skipping along with a teddy bear in her arms, while her mother rushes to get back their coveted spot in the back corner they had to abandon for the restroom. The young girl has a smile on her lips while she hums "Old McDonald."

To be that free again…

How would that feel not to have a worry in the world, not to worry where your next meal will come from, to feel comforted and hugged by your parents? But I know better, even young, seemingly innocent young girls have things to worry about, even fear at night. I know some monsters are real.

Shaking my head to clear the thoughts that are rampant in my mind and the strange growing lump in my throat, I think about the others and what they're doing. My return, no doubt, may not matter as much to them as it does to me.

I'm dressed inconspicuously with my worn-out jeans and cotton pink shirt. My hair is thrown as an afterthought in a ponytail. My reading glasses hang heavily on my chest. My tennis shoes have seen better days.

I'm excited to be going back to Texas. It is home and comfort.

I had been on the hunt for a new marketing customer in Europe when the phone call came. I had just come off of an exhausting twelve hours of interviews and meetings. It had taken me three days to convince my staff that I had to get back to Texas by the end of the week. Even on the ride to the airport my personal assistant, Liz, who had loyally been with me for the past four years, had tried everything in her retinue to keep me there.

"Can you not stay just till the end of next week?"

"Can't this wait? What's going on?'

"Can we expect you back soon? Why won't you tell me?"

"No," had been my only reply to the barrage of questions Liz had flung at me in the last two days. Only after seeing me actually board the plane had she been convinced.

I take out the diary I've kept with me for the last fifteen years. I haven't read it since I shut it for the last time all those years ago. The memories are too painful. I have to force myself to read it now on the plane—have to remember all those horrible and wonderful memories, feelings, and torments. It's essential for me to remember since I'm going back.

On the intercom, a whiney, raspy female voice breaks into my thoughts and announces the boarding of my plane, and with anxiety suddenly at its peak, I reluctantly board the plane....